Fashioned from the Same Fabric

A 40-Day Devotional for Pastors' Wives

Volume One

Melissa D. West

Melissawest136@gmail.com

Printed in the United States of America

ISBN: 13 978-1-7356954-0-2

Acknowledgments

I would like to thank God, my Father, my Savior, my King, my Lord, for gifting me to express my heart on paper. He is the reason behind the gift.

To my husband, Kenneth, my pastor, priest, provider, protector, and earthly lord. Thank you for consistently loving me and taking care of me since the beginning of our marriage. You are a true man of God who passionately lives out each day according to God's word. Thank you for naming this Devotional and understanding the need for pastor's wives to encourage one another.

To my children, Kenneth Jr., Muriel, and Devon (my son in love), thank you for allowing me to complete this project and supporting me during the process. You are my heartbeats and my first ministry. I am proud of you and excited to see where the Lord will take you in life.

To my granddaughter Violet Grace, my little love, my legacy. You make my heart sing every day. I am so proud to be your grandmother.

My mother and grandmother, my mother Violet, thank you for giving me your sensitivity and a zeal to want to love life. My grandmother Sarah, who is with the Lord, thank you for being my source of foundation and strength.

To the matriarch of our family, Mildred, thank you for picking up the banter in keeping our family secure and alive.

To my spiritual mothers, First Lady Ida McBride and First Lady Pauline Taylor, thank you for showing me how to be true to myself.

Thank you for loving and accepting me as your First Lady to my Berean Bible Fellowship Church of Plano, Texas, family. I appreciate every experience that we have endured thus far. You are dear to my heart, and I love you.

Thank you for always loving and supporting me far and near to my family and friends, and you know who you are. You all have played a significant part in my development as a woman and as a believer in Christ.

To Jacqi Henry, Dana Bennett, Valencia Hunt, Tracie Bonnick, Michelle Brown, and Pastor James Hutchins. Thank you for editing and reading over the manuscript and for providing marketing and publishing information. Your knowledge and expertise are invaluable not only to me but to God's Kingdom.

To my fellow pastors' wives- this Devotional was written for you.

Thank you for an open mind and an understanding heart to all my readers as you read this Devotional. May it bless you to honor your pastor's wife for the rare jewel that she is.

Melissa West

CONTENTS

Foreword

I was so blessed to have the opportunity to read the devotional, *Fashioned from the same Fabric*, and to share my perspective as a pastor's wife for more than 32 years. I can say with certainty that Lady Melissa has pinned a beautifully written book of encouragement, prayer, and sisterhood. This work is a transparent glimpse into the heart of a pastor's wife.

In her pellucid style, Lady Melissa shares "behind the scene" moments while inviting our global pastors' wives to sit in this space with her. This book is literally a shared stroll through many of the joys, challenges, and matters of the heart, and at times, simply the issues of life that are unveiled through the lens of a pastor's wife! She engages the reader in an experience that invokes the feeling of a loving, supportive embrace. The experiences she relayed in her beautiful storytelling drew me into moments of our shared journey, some of which I commiserated with her as I read the pages. She touched some deep, painful places in my heart but never left me there! Lady Melissa always left me with a fresh imprint of God's Character and His Love on my heart! Other moments led me into beautiful worship, as she reflected on God's Love, Faithfulness, and Grace in The Call of The Pastor's Wife!

Lady Melissa's storytelling is endearing as she arrests our attention and takes us along on her day to day reflections and revelations of Divine Insight and Wisdom. Lastly, each reading is sealed with prayers of Divinely Empowered Submission and complete trust in God's Plan, God's Purpose, and God's Peace over this beautiful and unique sisterhood! We are sisters, beautifully *"Fashioned from the same Fabric!"*

Jacqi Bell Henry

Preface

I remember this day like it was yesterday. I was in my home sitting on the steps talking to a friend. During our conversation, I suddenly had a burning desire to serve Pastor's wives. I just wanted to be there for women like me to love them and show them their value. Why? Because this is something I so desperately needed. It was a Tuesday in February of 2014 when my heart was overwhelmed to serve pastors' wives. I asked the Lord how? How can I help them, and how can I show them how valuable they are?

At a women's retreat that our church hosted, I led a round table discussion about expectations as a pastor's wife and self-care. The panel was informative, but I felt as if I should be doing more, but what?

In August of 2014, I went through a season of discontent and disconnect. I am sure my sister, you can relate. A season where you feel worthless and useless. A season where it seems that all the good that you have tried to do is now met with quietness and blank stares. In September of 2014, after returning from a women's retreat I attended out of state, I returned home feeling lost. The Lord gently spoke to me and told me the reason for my discontent and disconnect was not for the reasons I thought. It was because I had taken my focus off Him. After I repented, I asked the Lord to lead me in a 40-day fast so that I could reconnect back with Him. During my fasting time, I wrote in my journal each day and was revived, refreshed, renewed, and restored.

I longed for every pastor's wife to experience a time of renewal with the Lord as I had. There were so many devotionals for women to read, but nothing was written explicitly for the pastor's wife. It was then the Lord inspired me to write a 40-day devotional speaking directly to the passage of a Pastor's wife.

This devotional, my sweet sister, was written with you in mind. It is my prayer that you will embrace each story as your own. May you find comfort and peace as you accept the fact that you matter so much to God and me.

Melissa

Dedication

This Devotional is lovingly dedicated to the memory of my mentor and friend, Dr. Lois Irene Evans. She was the epitome of grace and beauty. The Lord used her as a spiritual compass to lead and guide the pastor's wife on this uncharted journey. I will always love and cherish her because she saw value in someone who felt undervalued.

Day One

Stress Relief

For we are to God the pleasing aroma of Christ among those who are being
saved and those who are perishing.
2 Corinthians 2:15

Bath and Body Works carries an aromatherapy body care blend called "Stress Relief." They give several different aromas; Eucalyptus Spearmint, Eucalyptus Tea, and Eucalyptus Basil (that's one I haven't tried). The idea is to take a luxurious bath or a hot shower under hot running steamed water, squeeze out just a little of the bath oil or gel, and inhaled the scent until you feel your body go limp. The aroma of the fragrance is geared to uplift your spirits and clear your mind. After you towel off, then use the body lotion and midst to lock in the scent. As you go about your day, you will be uplifted, and your stress is relieved because you are constantly inhaling the aroma's fragrance. But what they do not tell us that as soon as we wash our hands or take a shower or a bath, the scent washes off, and we must re-apply it again to get the desired result.

I love the eucalyptus aroma. It gives off a calming effect and puts me in a place of solitude and comfort. But the one thing I must remind myself of is who created the eucalyptus stem. I must remember who gave me my nose to smell the aroma. I reflect on my ability to breathe and take in deep breaths to relax at the moment. I stay mindful of who created the steam from the water and who made the water.

My heart melts when I think about how God's creation proves that He is always thinking of me. He still provides peace for me when I feel stressed and when I need the world to stop.

His love for us is unique because He provides fragrances from the earth that He created to enjoy. He tells us in 2 Corinthians 2:15 that we are a fragrance of Christ to Him!

Stress can be overwhelming at times in our lives, but knowing that we are fragrant of Christ to the Father should give us the stress relief we need. It is the kind of comfort that will never wash off or fade away. It is the kind of relief that we do not have to buy because the blood of Jesus has purchased us. It is the kind of relief that we can find comfort and peace even amid stressful situations.

Father,

Thank You for being our stress relief. Thank You for seeing us as a pleasant smell to Your nostrils through the blood of Your Son, Jesus. We are humbled and grateful that You think so much of us, even when we were stinking in sin. But because of our accepting You in our lives, we became an aroma that has pleased You. We bless and honor Your name. Amen!

Day One

Patches to Stitch to my Life

_____

_____

_____

_____

_____

_____

_____

_____

_____

_____

_____

_____

_____

_____

_____

_____

_____

_____

_____

_____

_____

_____

_____

Fashion your thoughts on these:

James 1:2-4

John 14:27

Romans 16:20

Day Two

Recall Notice

For everything, there is a season,
a time for every activity under heaven.
Ecclesiastes 3:1

Tedral is a medication that I began taking as a child to control my asthma symptoms. I used this medication for many years until I had my second child in 1993. After I took the drug and it had a chance to settle in my bloodstream, it would cause tremors. My heart rate would increase, and it put me in a daze. In addition to this, it would upset my stomach, and it also made me very sleepy. Even though I experienced the side effects, I was not concerned. It was a temporary fix to what seemed to be a permanent problem. There is a saying that I have heard all my life, "If it's not broken, then don't fix it."

The pharmaceutical market did not see it that way. They pulled it off the shelf after many years on the market. They claimed, Tedral was a highly addictive drug that contained phenobarbital. I thought to myself, *Really?! After all these years of taking this medication to control my asthma symptoms, NOW you tell me that you recalled due to its high probability of me becoming addicted to it.* But the truth was, I did depend on it, maybe more than I needed to because it worked, or so I thought. I did not care that the recall was for my good. I did not want to go through finding another medication that would combat my asthma symptoms. I was satisfied with what I had, regardless of the harmful side effects.

What has the Lord called recalled in your life? What did He have to pull off the shelf in your life so that you may become a more effective pastor's wife? Was it a toxic relationship that was causing harmful side effects? Did He recall a ministry in which you had become too comfortable? Did He recall a situation you thought you could handle? Did He remember parts of your personality that you did not want to change because you were comfortable being who you were?

We cannot get too comfortable with anything that the Lord gives us because seasons will change. His plan for us is to grow and learn more of His ways so that we can prosper in the plans He has for our lives. Trust that the Lord must issue recall notices in our lives to shake us, prune us, and grow us. We cannot remain where we are and fulfill the divine plan He has for our lives. Allow Him to recall everything in your life that needs to change so that you can be blessed beyond all that you can imagine or think. I promise you; He recalls so that He can renew.

Father,

Teach me to trust You as You recall those things in my life that does not mean me any good. Remove everything that I want to hold on to because I have simply gotten comfortable. Help me to see that recall from You is a powerful thing because it will cause me to seek You as my enduring hope to temporary circumstances. Your Word tells us that You know the plans you have for us, plans to prosper us and not harm us and bring us to an expected end. Help us to see Lord, that recalls are necessary for us to thrive as our souls prosper. In Your name, we pray, Amen!

Day Two

Patches to Stitch to my Life

_____

_____

_____

_____

_____

_____

_____

_____

_____

_____

_____

_____

_____

_____

_____

_____

_____

_____

_____

_____

_____

_____

_____

_____

_____

_____

_____

Fashion your thoughts on these:

2 Corinthians 5:17

Isaiah 43:19

Romans 12: 1-2

Meet with Me

> But the LORD said to Samuel, "Do not consider his appearance or his height, for I have rejected him. The LORD does not look at the things people look at. People look at the outward appearance, but the LORD looks at the heart."
>
> *1 Samuel 16: 7*

Beautiful lady, your role is a unique and delicate one. You may not only have the honor of serving as the First Lady of your church, but you also may be the leader of your women's ministry. You are often pulled in many directions, from calling emergency meetings to sitting and praying with the daughters of the house who are in distress.

In our women's ministry, the Lord impressed on my heart in October 2011 to have a one on one fellowship with each lady in our church. He spoke those words to me as we were preparing to close out bible study. Right before the prayer began, the Lord thundered, *Meet with each lady one on one.* I turned around where I was standing to see if someone was behind me who had spoken those words. My husband, Kenneth, strangely looked at me, so I whispered that I would explain it to him later.

I immediately started setting up one on one fellowships with each lady in our church, at restaurants, their homes, or meeting them at Starbucks. I began to understand slowly why the Lord told me to do this. These fellowships gave them a chance to learn more about me, and in return, I would know more about them. It gave them a sense of belonging and feeling *genuinely loved* by their First Lady. During these fellowships, many of them told me that they never had a Pastor's wife to do anything like this before. They never had someone to take time and learn about each one of them. They shared things with me that, typically, they would not have shared. They loved the idea of their Pastor's wife being so personable and available.

Dear sister, we must make it a heart thing. We are regularly misunderstood, and that could be because no one knows our hearts. This thinking can go both ways for the ladies that we serve in our church. Some we see with frowns constantly on their faces, and some smile all the time because they do not want you to see them being ingenuine or in pain. Some gripe about every little thing, some are timid if you look at them, some never have a kind word to say to you, and some will go out of their way to please you. Sometimes, all it takes is you saying, "Let's fellowship together, just you and I." The only way to genuinely understand each lady's heart is to say, "Meet with me."

Father,

We know that it is not always easy to get to know and understand a person. But this role that You have called us to is a unique one. We are continually called to come out of our comfort zones. We are called to love and protect the daughters You have put in our care. Help us, dear Father, to see these delicate souls as You see them. Show us, Lord, how to break down the walls of stone that many of them hide behind because of the fear of being hurt. And as we meet with them, Lord, we ask that You protect our hearts and give us wise counsel as we share with each one You have put in our care. In your name, we pray, Amen!

Day Three

Patches to Stitch to my Life

_____
_____
_____
_____
_____
_____
_____
_____
_____
_____
_____
_____
_____
_____
_____
_____
_____
_____
_____
_____
_____
_____
_____
_____
_____
_____

Fashion your thoughts on these:

Ezekiel 36:26

Luke 6:45

Psalm 139:1-5

A Blank Slate

For we are God's handiwork, created in Christ Jesus to do good works, which God prepared in advance for us to do.
Ephesians 2:10

All through my house are canvases with beautiful artwork painted on them. Do you ever sit and wonder what the artist must have been thinking when he painted the pictures in your home?

I imagine the artist sitting and thinking about how they will place their vision onto the blank slate sitting in front of them. They close their eyes, and then, they open them. They stare at the slate because they know that their sketch must be one that best demonstrates their style. They know that once their brush touches the slate, there is no going back.

Now, they are ready to create their masterpiece. They pick up the brush, and they paint each stroke as they envision it. Each stroke is carefully detailed, and each color is blending perfectly. Their head slightly turns as they continue to paint their image of perfection. They are focused because there is no room for mistakes. They paint, smile, stop, examine, and then with a sigh of satisfaction, their portrait is complete- finally, a lovely picture to be admired by many.

When we became Pastors' wives, many of us did not see ourselves as a blank slate. We started painting our image or let others paint a picture of how a pastor's wife is viewed. Some of us may have started painting the slate by stepping into roles in our church that we were not called to do. Some of us allowed the brush to stroke in the same place we have seen other pastor's wives serve. We did not see ourselves as a beautiful image formed in the mind of God and His expectation of us.

When God called us to this role, He had already painted the slate for us. His image of us is not the same but serves the same purpose. All of us cannot be pianists, organists, soloists, work in children's church, teach Sunday school, or be administrative assistants. We can only be what the Lord has purposed us to be and to do what He has called us to do. That is what makes us so unique. If God is leading us, each slate will have a different picture. Allow Him to paint the canvas of your role as a Pastor's wife. Your image will reflect its originality and beauty as the Lord intended for it to be.

Father,

Help us to get out of our way and get in Your way. We sometimes get ahead of ourselves, maybe because we want to please You, or we get the idea in our heads that this is what a Pastor's wife should be doing. You have done the calling, and we have answered. Let us sit still as You paint each purpose You have for our lives. You are the Master Artist, and You are incapable of making mistakes. Help us trust You as You guide us in this journey. In Your name, and we pray, Amen!

Day Four

Patches to Stitch to my Life

_____

_____

_____

_____

_____

_____

_____

_____

_____

_____

_____

_____

_____

_____

_____

_____

_____

_____

_____

_____

_____

_____

_____

_____

Fashion your thoughts on these:

Genesis 1:27

Genesis 1:31

Job 33:4

Weight Is Not Your Friend

Cast all your anxiety on him because he cares for you.
1 Peter 5:7

Please believe me. I am not meddling. I know that many of us struggle with our weight! But I do know that behind every weight problem is a story. Here is mine:

In February 2005, I experienced a loss; my heart could not reconcile, my childhood friend's death. She and I had been best friends, more like sisters, since we were ages five and six years old. This season was hard for me, and I simply did not know what to do with the emotions that penetrated my soul.

In April of 2005, I had a relapse of a chronic condition that I toil with from time to time called CIU, better known as Chronic Idiopathic Urticaria, or chronic hives. It is a painful and irritating condition that causes the skin to break out in small to large wheals or bumps that itch indescribably. It is a debilitating condition that can cause one to become withdrawn or depressed. My doctor prescribed a type of steroid, prednisone, to control the breakouts. The prednisone did its' job in managing the breakouts, but the medication's side effects were horrible. The higher dosage made the side effects more profound. It caused me to have a moon face, a humpback, swelling in my extremities, and my weight increased by 50 to 60 pounds! My height is 5 feet, 11 inches, my average weight is 170 to 175lbs, and now, here I am, averaging over 200 pounds! Emotional eating became my source of comfort and peace. Food allowed me to escape my pain and sorrow temporarily.

I could not stand for long periods. My legs and knees would hurt, and I could not walk without losing my breath. My blood pressure and sugar levels were rising because of the added weight. I remember thinking that if the doctors did not find a solution quickly, I could not continue living like this. I hated myself.

When the Lord delivered me from that season of my life, I remember looking back and asking myself what I learned from it? I knew that God had given me a heart and more compassion for overweight women and their struggles. He showed me that they are beautiful and that we should never make unfair assumptions because we don't know what people struggle with internally. I learned that I am not meant to carry the unnecessary weight of this world on my shoulders because I have a King who will do that for me. I learned that I was focusing too much on my struggle instead of what the battle would do for my character. When I felt that I could not go on, the Lord showed me that I could if I just surrendered my cares to Him.

Sister, it is the Lord's intention for us to cast our burdens and cares on Him. We all have been designed to bear so much, but not more than we can take. I know that a massive rock of spiritual warfare can make you feel heavy and helpless. When the stone is bearing down on us, and it seems that it might overtake us, the Lord steps in the right time and blocks the permanent damage it can cause. In your ministry, there will be many rocks, but rest assured that the Lord will not allow permanent damage to hinder your work for others. And when He removes the foundation of oppression from you, ask yourself, what have I learned from this season, and how can I grow from it.

Father,

Help us to know that if we allow You to remove the weight and cares of this world off our shoulders, our hearts become lighter, our steps towards righteousness become swifter, our energy to work in Your kingdom becomes exciting, and our minds are free to embrace all the great plans You have for us. Thank You, Lord, for being the ultimate weight reducer. In Your perfect name, I pray, Amen!

Day Five

Patches to Stitch to my Life

_____
_____
_____
_____
_____
_____
_____
_____
_____
_____
_____
_____
_____
_____
_____
_____
_____
_____
_____
_____
_____
_____
_____
_____
_____

Fashion your thoughts on these:

Psalm 68:19

Psalm 9:9

Psalm 55:22

Day Six

Do They Pray for Me?

I urge, then, first of all, that petitions, prayers, intercession, and thanksgiving be
made for all people
1 Timothy 2:1

"Father God, I come to You on bended knee and bowed down,
thanking You Lord, for Your many blessings. I 'wanna' thank You,
Lord, because You have been so very good to me and my family. Lord,
I want to pray and thank You for my pastor. Bless him, Lord, as he
leads Your people and teaches the flock Your everlasting Word. Lord,
bless the ministers, their wives, the deacons and their wives. Lord,
bless the church that we may serve You in spirit and in truth, in
Jesus's name, I pray, Amen."

Have you ever heard a prayer like that, or one similar to it, and
thought to yourself, did they forget someone? Me! Do they think that
I do not need prayer, or do they feel that I am some sort of invisible
entity? Do they not see that I am the one who upholds this man of
God that they are lifting in prayer? I often see and hear things because
I am married to the pastor. My shoulders get massive, too, because
not only do I uphold and comfort my husband, their pastor, my pastor,
but I must support the shoulders of others as well. How many times
have I changed my spiritual shoulder pads because they often wear
out due to the amount of wear and tear put on them? Lord, can you
please tell them I need prayer too. My heart aches for it; my soul
bleeds for it. Pray for me to stay healthy to support your pastor, my
pastor, as he leads the flock that God has entrusted to him.

It can be disheartening at times when we feel we are so often
neglected in prayer. However, the most fantastic thing that we can

realize is that Jesus prays for us all the time! Isn't that comforting to know? You, beloved, are always on His mind, all the time.

Romans 8:34 tells us, "It is Christ Jesus, who died, who was raised, who is at the right hand of God, who intercedes for us." Not only did He die and was raised from the dead, which is the perfect gift He gave us, but even after that great sacrifice, the verse comes back and tells us that He prays for us. We should always let our minds rest in this daily. The One who called us to this work is the same One who prays for us as we work.

Father,

It can be hard at times when we feel we are often neglected in the prayers of others. But thank You so much for Your abiding love and Your Word. You have expressed to us that You pray for us all the time. It gives us incredible strength and incomprehensible love. Teach us, Father, to shift our focus from an earthly to a spiritual transformation so that we can allow ourselves to be free from men and open in You. We love You so much, and we thank You for the precious gift of Your prayers for us. In Your name, we pray, Amen!

Day Six

Patches to Stitch to my Life

_____

_____

_____

_____

_____

_____

_____

_____

_____

_____

_____

_____

_____

_____

_____

_____

_____

_____

_____

_____

_____

_____

_____

_____

_____

_____

_____

_____

_____

Fashion your thoughts on these:

1 Timothy 2:1

Hebrews 7:25

Romans 8:26

Day Seven

Do I have to Lord

So now I am giving you a new commandment: Love each other. Just as I have loved you, you should love each other.
John 13:34.

Have you ever heard this statement before, "to know me is to love me?" I did not realize how foolish this statement was until I became a pastor's wife! I wonder, sometimes, do people think about the words that come out of their mouths?! How blatantly arrogant it is to make such an assumption that when I know you, I will automatically love you. I hear from my unauthorized spiritual advisors that I must show love all the time, whether it is reciprocated or not. I am thinking in the back of my mind, and *you can only be concerned with yourself while I must express this incredible love to many.*

Do you feel this way sometimes? Do you ever ask the Lord in your private moments with Him, do I have to Lord? Do I have to show them, love when they look at me, cross-eyed? Do I have to show them, love when they have imagined that I have said something negative about them only to find out I was misunderstood? Do I have to show them love, Lord, when I am purposely shunned? Do I have to show them love when I am lied to, and they don't apologize? Do I have to show them, love when they hurt me after I have been there for them when no one else was, only to be betrayed?

We know the answer to that, don't we, sister? Yes, we must show them love all the time despite how we feel and what they have done or have not done. We are not humanly capable of delivering and giving love away until we understand how much the Father loves us. When I think about how many times I have betrayed the Lord, I have shunned Him, how I have lied to Him and did not apologize right away for it. Or how I sinned before I became a believer and even after I became one. When I don't commune with Him, I fail to study and meditate on His Word, or I am selfish.

It humbles my heart and soul to know that a righteous God has loved me through all my unrighteousness. Yes, dear sister, it is challenging to love difficult people, especially those entrusted to us. His commandment is to love one another as He loves us.

Father,

There are times I want to give up because the challenges in ministry can be difficult. But we were Yours before we became theirs, and You loved us when we were unlovable. Thank You for humbling our hearts and convicting our souls of what must be done. Even now, You love us when we allow negative emotions to overcome the goodness that You have placed in us. Help us to remember that You are not the epitome of love, but You are love. Thank You once again for showing us that through You, we can love anyone. In Your name, we pray, Amen!

Day Seven

Patches to Stitch to my Life

_____

_____

_____

_____

_____

_____

_____

_____

_____

_____

_____

_____

_____

_____

_____

_____

_____

_____

_____

_____

_____

_____

_____

_____

Fashion your thoughts on these:

1 Peter 4:8

Romans 12:10

1 John 3:18

Day Eight

Red Light, Green Light

Dear friends, do not believe everyone who claims to speak by the Spirit. You must test them to see if the spirit they have comes from God. For there are many false prophets in the world.
1 John 4:1

Red Light, Green Light, was a popular childhood game I use to play. According to Wikihow.com; *When playing the game, one player is chosen to be the stoplight, and the other players of the game line up about 15 feet away from this person. The game starts when the person in the stoplight's role starts reciting, "Greenlight," and the players begin to advance toward the stoplight. The stoplight then turns around and says, "Red light," and the players stop in their tracks. The winner of the game is the one who reaches the stoplight first. Then they get to be the stoplight.* In this game, I have witnessed some people moving even when the stoplight is calling out red, and they often must go back to the starting point. This person disqualifies themself because they did not grasp the game's concept, which is to obey the commands of the Stop Light.

I've often wondered in our work how many times The Lord, our stoplight, has said red light to us. As pastors' wives, we want to do our best while serving in this role. We want to help soothe aching hearts and comfort troubling minds. We want to give our hearts to those who desperately need someone just to be there and love them. Sometimes, even our good intentions can be spoken of evilly. These are the times our Father is holding up the red-light sign, or He is whispering it in our hearts, do not advance on this one. The question is, do we listen to that voice, or do we proceed even if the light is red? How many times have we disqualified ourselves simply because we did not obey His voice or follow His command to stop at the red light?

Ministry involves discernment. When God called us to this ministry, He equipped us with a tool called *wisdom*. 1 Thessalonians 5:21-22 says: "But examine everything carefully; hold fast to that which is good; abstain from every form of evil." The apostle John issues a similar warning when he says, "Do not believe every spirit but test the spirits to see whether they are from God because many false prophets have gone out into the world." 1John 4:1.

In every situation we encounter, we must use discernment, which is our red light. If we proceed after the red-light warning has been issued, the outcome could be disastrous and may affect our ability to serve effectively in the future. Before we attempt to move forward in any situation, we must listen carefully to see if God is saying red light or green light, then proceed as directed by the Holy Spirit.

Father,

Help us, Lord, because we have hearts that want to serve You. Sometimes when we look at people, we see "help me" written all over them. We want to give them our time and our love. We want to hold them close to our hearts. But sometimes, we miss the red-light warning coming from You. We know that the enemy knows our good intentions, and he will try to trick us by coming in a tender-hearted disguise. Help us listen to that individual tool call wisdom and act on it because it is our green light. Help us to trust You when You say, red light, stop. We know that You are God Almighty, and You can see far beyond what we see. Help us to put our total trust in You. In Your matchless name, we pray, Amen!

Day Eight

Patches to Stitch to my Life

_____

_____

_____

_____

_____

_____

_____

_____

_____

_____

_____

_____

_____

_____

_____

_____

_____

_____

_____

_____

_____

_____

_____

Fashion your thoughts on these:

John 16:13

Romans 8:26

Psalm 143:10

Day Nine

The Silent Killer

*Be alert and of sober mind. Your enemy the devil prowls around like a roaring
lion looking for someone to devour.*
1 Peter 5:8

Hypertension. What is it? When we are diagnosed with Hypertension, we are recognized as having high blood pressure. According to Mayoclinic.org, this disease's stages *are broken down into four categories: Normal, Stage 1, Stage 2, and danger Zone!* The effects that high blood pressure can have on the body can be devastating if left untreated. Some who suffer from this disease must be medicated while experiencing unbelievable side effects, while others may manage it with a healthy diet, proper weight management, and exercise.

So why is it considered the silent killer? Because so many of us walk around, not realizing that our blood pressure is high or in the danger zone. We walk around, thinking all is well when we are heart attacks and strokes waiting to happen. While we are walking around feeling good and assuming all is well, this silent killer is damaging our bodies, a time bomb waiting to explode inside us. Why does this happen? Because we do not monitor our blood pressure, we consistently divulge poor eating habits, we do not manage our weight, and we do not exercise. We assume that since we feel well, there is no need to change our existing habits. Here is this adage I have previously mentioned before; *"If it's not broken, don't fix it."* Maybe another statement should be, *"Are we always aware of when something inside of us is broken?"*

In the spiritual realm, we have a silent killer, and his name is Satan! He is going to and fro seeking whom he may devour, 1 Peter 5:8. My precious sister, the bible says that he is our GREAT accuser going around like a roaring lion. According to David Guzik, a bible commentator, *"For Christians, Satan is a lion who may roar but who has been de-fanged at the cross (Colossians 2:15). Yet the sound of his roar - his deceptive lies are still potent, and he has the power to devour souls and rob Christians of effectiveness.*

Dear sister, The Lord has provided us with spiritual tools that show us how to stay alert and spiritually healthy. We have a monitor, which is the Holy Spirit. And believe me, it works if we keep Him near us. In the spiritual realm, we have a nutritious diet, which is His precious Word. Let us feast on it daily so that we can stay fit and ready to fight. And the way we exercise in the spiritual realm is through faith and praying. When we pray to the Father, we must believe when we pray and put that faith in a movement mode. If we do these things, we will never be caught unaware, and Satan's power over us becomes impotent and powerless.

Father,

Thank You for Your divine protection from an enemy we cannot see. We know that He is invisible in our physical realm waiting to pounce on us at any given time. But we are so grateful that You remind us often to check our spiritual monitor so that we will be able to see that danger is approaching. Help us stay connected to the monitor, feast on your Word, and activate our faith through prayer. We thank You for Your invisible protection, Father. Show us how to render the enemy powerless over our circumstances. In Your Holy Name, Amen!

Day Nine

Patches to Stitch to my Life

_____

_____

_____

_____

_____

_____

_____

_____

_____

_____

_____

_____

_____

_____

_____

_____

_____

_____

_____

_____

_____

_____

_____

Fashion your thoughts on these:

2 Corinthians 4:4

John 10:10

Ephesians 4:27

Day Ten

Healer of Hearts

I am reminded of your sincere faith, which first lived in your grandmother Lois and in your mother Eunice and, I am persuaded, now lives in you also.
2 Timothy 1:5

On April 9, 2016, my life as I had known it changed forever. At 2:27 am, I awoke to a phone call informing me that my dear sweet grandmother had gone into cardiac arrest and passed away. I can still hear the nurse telling me this as I struggled to fully awake and understand what she said: *'Mrs. West, I am sorry to inform you that Mrs. Griffin passed away.'* Her voice slowly started to sound like a gurgle of wind coming from the clouds as I began to process the fact that 'Momma' was gone. With Momma being 91 years old, I knew the possibility of this day coming would be sooner rather than later due to her recent health challenges. But who is ever ready, regardless of how old they are, to let them go? I certainly was not.

During the preparation of her home-going celebration services, I kept hearing over and over in my head and my heart, God, is a "healer of hearts." But being in the depth of my grief and sorrow, I thought to myself, *yeah right.* As the weeks began to pass by, I became aware that God is indeed a healer of hearts. My thoughts of Momma and everything she imparted in me slowly started to eat away at my grief. A dear friend said these words to me after she had recently experienced death in her family; "Remember everything that she put inside of you. Remember the sweet and precious memories. Remember, she raised you to be the woman that you are today, and you are imparting those seeds that she gave to you, to your children, and the ladies of your church." Without her knowing this, a shift in my heart took place immediately.

My dear sister, how does God heal the heart? By reminding us of what He has already put inside of us. Perhaps, you have just recently experienced or have been coping with the death of a loved one who meant so very much to you: your mother, your grandmother, an aunt, or someone who raised you. The pain in your life is unbearable, and you need a release. The Lord wants you to remember why He gave them to you in the first place. To plant seeds of life in you so that you can grow in your faith and impart those same seeds in someone else. Remember, dear one, your Lois or Eunice may be gone, but you have just become a Lois or a Eunice to someone else. Gird up, girlfriend! Impart those seeds of life and faith to your children, and the daughters of your church, that the Lord has entrusted to you.

Father,

Thank You for speaking to us through Your Word and through the people that You give us in this season. Thank You for the sweet and gentle reminders that You alone are the Healer of our hearts. Thank You, Lord, for the time we had our Lois's and our Eunice's because we know that what they have imparted in us, we will continue that legacy and impart the seeds of faith in those you have entrusted to us. Help us to walk worthy of that calling, Lord. And when our hearts become sad, gently remind us that You are our healer and lead us back to this place of comfort. In Your Holy and Matchless Name, I pray, Amen!

Day Ten

Patches to Stitch to my Life

_____

_____

_____

_____

_____

_____

_____

_____

_____

_____

_____

_____

_____

_____

_____

_____

_____

_____

_____

_____

_____

_____

_____

_____

_____

Fashion your thoughts on these:

Psalm 34:18

Matthew 5:4

Revelation 21:4

The Invisible Me

Worship the LORD with gladness; come before him with joyful songs.
Know that the LORD is God. It is he who made us, and we are his; we are his
people, the sheep of his pasture.
Psalm 100:2-3

Scenario One: "Excuse me, how are you today, sister?" *Oh, I guess she did not see me standing right here next to my husband. But how can she miss me since I am standing near 6"0 feet tall!* Scenario Two: "Oh, hi, Sister, my, that is a lovely dress you are wearing this morning." *Oh, I guess she only saw the lady I was in a deep conversation with when she walked up, interrupted us, and took her away.* Scenario Three: "Well, hello, ladies, and how are you this fine morning?" *Wow, am I invisible? Did they not hear me greet them just now?*

Dear heart, do you feel this way sometimes? Do you feel like an alien dropped off on the wrong planet? Or do you honestly feel like someone hidden behind a glass wall? You know that you are visible, but they treat you as if you are invisible. I know what that feels like, and I am sure that you do too.

We have been purposely called NOT to fit in. And sometimes, not fitting in will make us seem like we are invisible in the church. Truthfully, that statement could not be more wrong because we are very visible whether we want to be or not. The enemy is regularly playing games with our minds and our spirits. It is his job to make us feel inadequate and disconnected in our calling. He is cunning and shifty, and he will use people to make us feel worthless.

We may ask the Lord, "how can I serve a people like this, Lord when they treat me as if I am a cat hair hidden in a piece of fur?" How can I minister to these ladies when it seems that I am continually being disrespected or blatantly ignored? Well, let me tell you how:

When we truly focus on serving the Lord with gladness and not focus on whether people speak to us or not, His word puts us in a different mind space that will allow us to be glad in our service to Him. We are sheep that have been called out to serve Him in this role and this capacity. But if our flesh interferes with our serving, we cannot be glad in what we do. The one thing we can count on, dear sister, we are not invisible to the Almighty God, our Father in heaven. And His assurance is all that we need.

Father,

Thank You for the way of escape when we go to Your Word. You remind us all the time to keep our hearts and minds focused on You. But Lord, we must admit, sometimes it is difficult to do that when we allow people to enter a space that only belongs to You. Help us to retreat to our secret place where only You dwell with us so that we can be reminded that we will serve You, and we will be glad about it. In Your name, Amen!

Day Eleven

Patches to Stitch to my Life

_____

_____

_____

_____

_____

_____

_____

_____

_____

_____

_____

_____

_____

_____

_____

_____

_____

_____

_____

_____

_____

_____

_____

_____

Fashion your thoughts on these:

Proverbs 17:22

Proverbs 15:13

Mark 10:45

You will Live and not Die

I will not die but live,
and will proclaim what the LORD has done.
Psalm 118:17

In 2004, we had two trees planted in our front yard when the house was built, which is usually a standard in most developing neighborhoods in the Texas suburbs. The tree that was planted on the left side of the front yard sprouted quickly and started growing. However, the tree on the front yard's right side remained as it was when it was planted. Year after year, season after season, my husband, Kenneth, and I watched this tree stay in a dormant state. Every year a few leaves would sprout on the branches in the spring, but nothing more. It was as if the tree was satisfied with its present state and decided to remain there. Kenneth and I decided that maybe we should just cut our loss, have it cut down, and plant a new tree in its place.

Then in the spring of 2015, we noticed the tree on the left side of the yard stopped growing and died almost immediately. We were shocked because its demise seemed to just come out of nowhere. However, our dormant tree on the right side of the yard started proliferating. It was as if someone breathed the breath of life into it, and it began to sprout more leaves and grow taller. In 2017, Kenneth cut the dead branches off our dormant tree to see if it would continue to grow, and it did! Today, it is taller than our house and still growing! The tree that was flourishing in the beginning stop growing and eventually died. However, the tree we were about to give up on and cut down began growing by leaps and bounds. It appeared that there was no life in it, but it proved us wrong. It needed more time to be alone to recalibrate, take root, and heal itself before growth could take place.

Perhaps your ministry, in the beginning, was like our tree on the left side of the front yard. I know our church was! It had taken root and started growing immediately. It was flourishing in season and out of season. But then suddenly, the growth came to a standstill. Leaves withered, branches dried up, and it appeared that the root was dying. It seems that it was only producing enough to sustain itself like the tree on the front yard's right side. We see a little movement, but not much on the surface seems to be going in a growth direction. We have often thought, maybe we should just cut our losses, give it up, and move on to another assignment. However, God has shown us too much for us to give up now. We have seen miracles, after miracles, happening at our branch of Zion. Father has shown us that the root is not dead, and it will live and not die.

Dear one, encourage your *pastor, husband,* not to give up. The branches will start sprouting again. Trust God and leave the ministry in His hands. He is the Master Healer and Restorer, and He will recalibrate your ministry again! It took 11 years for our tree on the right side of the yard to take root and grow! In the meantime, cut off the ministry's dead branches so the healthy ones can spring forth and grow taller.

Father,

Thank You for letting us know that You have the last say so. You not only planted the tree, but You will root it and grow it in due season. In Your name, I pray, Amen!

Day Twelve

Patches to Stitch to my Life

_____
_____
_____
_____
_____
_____
_____
_____
_____
_____
_____
_____
_____
_____
_____
_____
_____
_____
_____
_____
_____
_____
_____
_____

Fashion your thoughts on these:

Jeremiah 17:8

Ephesians 3:20

Psalm 1:3

The Leaping Squirrel

I lift up my eyes to the mountains where does my help come from?
My help comes from the LORD, the Maker of heaven and earth.
Psalm 121: 1-2

I love walking in my neighborhood. As I take in God's scenery, I appreciate His majestic power even more. I enjoy seeing quite a few furry friends with bushy tails leaping from one place to another in our community. This morning, as I was walking, I was swiftly approaching one of my fuzzy tail friends. When he realized how fast I was coming towards him, without thinking, he leaped from the sidewalk to the nearest tree and scurried up as quickly as he could. I was a symbol of danger in his mind, and he knew that he would be safe if he went up.

How many of us, dear sister, think as a squirrel does? Does our faith leap up when danger approaches? Do we scurry around looking for a place to run, or do we look up knowing that *we will be safe if we can go high*?

That squirrel was smart enough to get out of my way by leaping up and staying up until I had gotten out of its way. The danger is always around us, and we cannot escape it. There are dangers seen and unseen. Being on the front line, we are always surrounded by danger. Dangerous people who try to get close to us with ill intentional motives, people who scheme and plot behind our backs while smiling in our faces--- these people approach us with the intent of killing our spirit. But when danger is upon us, our faith needs to leap high to the hills because our only chance of escaping is through the Lord.

Father,

Proverbs 22:3 says, A prudent person foresees danger and takes precautions. The simpleton goes blindly on and suffers the consequences. Help us always to be alert and looking for a way up when danger approaches us. Speak your word clearly to our hearts so that we will know how to escape the enemy when he comes to assassinate our character and shoot down our spirits. May we leap high in You knowing that if we do, we will be safe. Thank You always for Your divine protection. In Your matchless name, I pray, Amen!

Day Thirteen

Patches to Stitch to my Life

_____
_____
_____
_____
_____
_____
_____
_____
_____
_____
_____
_____
_____
_____
_____
_____
_____
_____
_____
_____
_____
_____
_____
_____
_____
_____
_____

Fashion your thoughts on these:

Deuteronomy 31:6

2 Thessalonians 3:3

Psalm 32:7

The One

The LORD God said, "It is not good for the man to be alone. I will make a helper suitable for him."
Genesis 2:18

Who is she? Can you point her out to me? I am looking for a woman who is wearing a pretty dress, shoes, purse, and hat to match. I am looking for a woman who is dignified and walks with an "air" about her. I am looking for a charming lady who is always smiling when she walks into the sanctuary. I am looking for the one who always has it together. Is that her over there? Is she the one that is sitting pretty with the scarf draped over her legs? Oh no, that must be her over there, the one who is smiling so pretty and holding on to the pastor's arm. No, I guess that wasn't her either. I am so confused. Where is the leading lady of the church?

Allow me to tell you where she is; she is over there, cleaning the bathroom stalls while others walk in and out, speaking and smiling as she cleans them without asking if she needs help. She is the one washing the dirty dishes because she knows that guests will be attending service today, and she wants everything to be tidy and clean. She is the one praying on the altar alone because she wants the sanctuary to be sanctified and consecrated before worship service begins. She is the one wearing a pretty suit. Her suit reflects the stain and soil of one of her daughter's tears, who shared that her marriage is ending. She is the one holding the baby of the woman holding the arm of the pastor for strength. She is the one with her head down, praying for her husband as he preaches God's Word and encouraging him in her silence.

You see, the leading lady leads by example! She is the one God handpicked to stand in the gap for the pastor because He knew the man of God would need a strong woman full of grace, courage, and humility to cover him. She is the one who is seldom appreciated, hardly recognized for the good she does, usually talked negatively about, overlooked by pastor pleasers, under-valued, the one who bites her tongue amid adversity so that she won't taint the witness of her husband, the one filling in the gaps wherever necessary so that service can run smoothly. She is the one called to be a mother to many daughters, a grandmother to babies who need one, a friend, a counselor, an encourager, a supporter, the one who is never expected to get tired. God chose her, shaped her, tested her, protected her, molded her, pruned her, and set her apart because He wanted her to be the ONE, a Pastor's Wife!

Father,

To be a pastor's wife is truly humbling. Thank You for gifting us, molding us, pruning us, and trusting us even before our limbs were formed together in our mother's womb. It is a lonely, consuming, and often overwhelming call; however, it is reassuring to know that You chose us, handpicked us to stand beside our husbands for such a time as this. Thank You for reminding us that it is You who keeps us secured and safely in Your arms. It is You who chose us as the one who would fulfill this purpose in our lives for the benefit of Your Kingdom. In Your name, I pray, Amen!

Day Fourteen

Patches to Stitch to my Life

_____

_____

_____

_____

_____

_____

_____

_____

_____

_____

_____

_____

_____

_____

_____

_____

_____

_____

_____

_____

_____

_____

_____

_____

Fashion your thoughts on these:

1 Timothy 3:11

Proverbs 31:10-31

Proverbs 12:4

Day Fifteen

Tickling the Ivories

Let us not become weary in doing good, for at the proper time we will reap a harvest if we do not give up.
Galatians 6:9

I love the piano. When I was ten years old, I begged my grandmother to let me take piano lessons, and she agreed. However, she did not purchase a piano for me until she saw that I was serious about continuing the classes. I remember when I was about 13 years old and had just gotten home from school. I walked into my bedroom, and there it was my beautiful upright piano! I remember smelling the newness of the wood and loving the sound that was coming from it. I vividly remember gliding my long fingers up and down those beautiful ivories. I would sit for hours and just practice because I loved learning new music and just merely tickling the ivories of my new piano and smelling the unique fragrance of the wood.

When I turned 15 years old, I began to lose interest in taking piano lessons. The newness had worn off, and I found myself becoming discontent and frustrated because the music was starting to get complicated. I had to work harder to master a new piece. By this time, I had other interests that I wanted to pursue, and I was just ready to quit and move on to something more comfortable and more practical. My grandmother quickly laid down the law and said to me, "You wanted to take lessons, I bought this piano for you, and you will continue to learn." She did not care about me complaining, not showing interest, or pouting. Her word was final, and I had no choice but to keep tickling those ivories, whether I wanted to or not.

When we are first called into this role alongside our husbands, we are excited because of the position's newness. We are eager to get started, so much so that we jump in with both feet leveled to the ground. Everything is so fresh and new that we can smell the ministry's wood's freshness and fragrance. After serving a few years, we are burned out, and we become resentful being the topic of household conversations. We become a bit weary when our sincere service is not reciprocated or appreciated. We tell God, "I'm not interested anymore in doing this Lord, and I want to quit." However, our Father gently reminds us that He did the calling, and we cannot just quit because we feel like it or because the newness has worn off. He tells us that we are to serve until He says it is time to move on to another assignment, or He calls us home to be with Him. Then He does something beautiful and pure by allowing us to remember the fragrance we once smelled when He first called us. This fragrance motivates us to keep working and serving.

Beautiful one, when we get tired or weary, remember if we continue to tickle the ivories and do not quit, we will eventually begin to make beautiful music in ministry again.

Father,

Ministry is beautiful because You designed it to be. However, there are times when the freshness has worn off that it can become tedious and overbearing. Thank You for reminding us that You are our Savior, Master, and Lord, and we are serving in this capacity because You called us. Help us always smell the wood's newness when we are down, feel belittled, or unappreciated. Please remind us that You give blessings, and we will reap the harvest if we don't give up. In Your name, I pray, Amen!!!

Day Fifteen

Patches to Stitch to my Life

_____
_____
_____
_____
_____
_____
_____
_____
_____
_____
_____
_____
_____
_____
_____
_____
_____
_____
_____
_____
_____
_____
_____

Fashion your thoughts on these:

Jeremiah 31:12

Isaiah 40:31

Hebrews 12:1-3

Day Sixteen

Hagar Alert

Now Sarai, Abram's wife, had borne him no children. But she had an
Egyptian slave named Hagar.
Genesis 16:1

As I was reading this passage, one of the things that stood out
to me besides the obvious was a woman with the title of a wife,
abdicating wifely privileges to a woman with the title of a servant.

In this day and time, titles mean a lot to some people. In other
words, people take on the character of the claim that they assume.
When I married my husband almost 30 years ago, I not only took his
name, but this became a part of my character. I went from being
Melissa Shelby to Melissa West. That meant I had all the rights and
privileges of being a West. I was privy to whatever my husband had
and offered me because I had characteristically assumed his name and
the position of being his wife. I also knew there was only room for
one woman to take his name, and no other woman then or now can
assume what was rightfully, legally, and spiritually given to me. My
character went from being single to becoming a helper. I am a helper
in every aspect of my marriage. *This* calling of being married to *this*
man was ordained by God and given to me. Now, when God sees us,
He sees one flesh, one mind, one heart, one soul, operating as one,
serving Him.

Why is it that when our husbands are called to be pastor's, we
willfully hand over our helping role to a foreign woman, an outsider?
When we allow foreigners to enter a covenant relationship with our
husbands, as was the case with Abram and Sarai, we are lighting a
fire that may not be so easy to fan out. God gives our pastor-husbands
a vision and a command to lead His people. He also gives his helper,
his wife, a charge to help bring the vision to life. If God does not

provide specific instructions on what woman to bring aboard to lead a ministry or to do particular work to aid the pastor, it will behoove us to pray and wait until He does. I have seen too many pastors' wives who hand their pastor-husbands' welfare over to a woman who was not included as a part of the covenant. As God gives our husbands the vision, our job is to wait on the visual manifestation and not hurry it along. Our job is to remain with him, stand by him, and trust God to do what He wants to be done for his kingdom.

Only you can fulfill what God has given you to achieve. It is not our place to find a replacement to fulfill a purpose that God has given to us. Now do not get me wrong; women can and should be encouraged to serve in ministry. I am merely saying, there is only one leading lady in your church, and that lady is you. When you, dear Sarai, invite a Hagar in to take on a role that was characteristically designed and assigned to you, she will despise and mistreat you because you put her in a place of authority over you. Keep your alert for a Hagar on high so that the work of the Lord will not be hindered.

Father,

Help us to remember to embrace Your plans for our ministries. Help us not hurry the vision that You have given to our husbands, but always trust the Supreme Visionary, which is You. Amen!

Day Sixteen

Patches to Stitch to my Life

_____

_____

_____

_____

_____

_____

_____

_____

_____

_____

_____

_____

_____

_____

_____

_____

_____

_____

_____

_____

_____

_____

_____

_____

Fashion your thoughts on these:

1 John 4:1

Habakkuk 2:3

John 15:16

Day Seventeen

Counting the Steps

Trust in the LORD with all your heart and lean not on your own understanding;
In all your ways submit to him, and he will make your paths straight.
Proverbs 3:5-6

I've mentioned that I love walking in my neighborhood. I love the peace it gives me and the much-needed exercise as well. If I am not able to go to the gym, I will briskly walk in my neighborhood.

On this particular morning, I made up in my mind that I would increase my work-out intensity by adding a light jog to my routine. I felt I had reached a plateau, so it was time to push myself to see what I could do. As I was making the last stretch of briskly walking back to my house, I decided to start jogging to test my endurance. As I began to jog, I looked in front of me and saw the distance of where I needed to get to, and I became discouraged. I remember saying to myself, "Girl, you are NOT going to make it!" Then I heard the Holy Spirit speak to me, as you jog, focus on each concrete slab. So, I took my focus off the distance and began to focus on each concrete slab. Before I knew it, I had made it to the finish line in record time. What amazed me the most is when I looked back, I saw how far I had come!

The Holy Spirit taught me a valuable lesson that morning. Often, we focus on the distance of our journey rather than going through the steps successfully. We get discouraged because we want to magically zoom from one area in our life to another without appreciating the journey stages.

Isn't this just like a ministry? We want the hard times to hurry up and be over. We make the mistake of looking too far down the road instead of focusing on the process of getting to where the Lord is taking us. When we look at the concrete slabs of ministry through our eyes, we get distressed and discouraged. But when we focus on the concrete slabs and look at them through the Master's eyes, He changes our perspective. He communes with us, He comforts our spirits, quietly calms us, energizes us, and before we know it, the process is complete, that journey has ended, and we are getting prepared for the next one.

Dear one, I know aspects of this journey can be overwhelming at times. And when we are in the middle of a crisis, looking down the road seems bleak and weary. I encourage you to focus on the slabs, pace yourself, and jog one step at a time. And while you are counting each step, pray and commune with your Heavenly Father.

Father,

Thank You for always nudging my heart to listen to You. How would I ever be able to make it without Your guidance? Sometimes I am deficient in spirit and weak at heart, but You are my sustainer and energizer. Help me, dear Lord, when I am in a crisis to focus and trust You. The enemy wants me to go through the trouble without being strengthened. You want me to be strengthened as I go through the process so that when I reach the finish line of that season, I will be able to withstand the next one. I honor You, Father, and I thank You for Your love. In the name of Jesus, Amen!

Day Seventeen

Patches to Stitch to my Life

_____

_____

_____

_____

_____

_____

_____

_____

_____

_____

_____

_____

_____

_____

_____

_____

_____

_____

_____

_____

_____

_____

_____

_____

_____

_____

Fashion your thoughts on these:

Philippians 4:13

1 Corinthians 1:8

Philippians 3:12

Day Eighteen

He needs your Covering

She brings him good, not harm,
all the days of her life.
Proverbs 31:12

He comes home after working a twelve-hour day in Corporate America. He speaks to let everyone in the house know that he is home. After putting the mail on the kitchen island, he goes into the bedroom and takes a nap. He then arises late in the evening to prepare for conference calls, upcoming church meetings, calendar updates from his admin, and schoolwork because he is studying to receive his master's degree. He will sneak in a meal at his desk as he checks on members he has not seen in weeks at worship service. After burning the midnight oil, he shuts down for the night only to be awakened by a church member that someone has passed away. So, he arises from bed, gets dressed, and goes to minister and console the family, putting aside that his day will begin in four hours.

He is usually the first one to arrive Sunday morning, making sure everything is in working order. He wants to make sure the building is warm or cold, depending on the season. He will sometimes stand at the front door, greeting members and guests as they arrive. He walks into the sanctuary to pray and meditate for the congregation. In his eyes, I can see the circumstances of the people that are mounted on his shoulders. He loves God's people so much that it drains him, especially when the love is not reciprocated or appreciated.

Does this sound familiar, dear one? All of this is only a droplet of what I see my husband do daily. He does so much more, as I am sure your pastor- husband does as well.

As wives of these called men of God, our first assignment is to cover them at all times in prayer. We are called to nurture, protect, honor, console, guard, and listen to him. We are to be his strength when he is weak and help carry his load when he is weighed down. We must be the salve when he is wounded and the shoulder that is always available when he needs comfort. We are not only his wife; we are his life partner in ministry; we are his covering!

Father,

Ministry is difficult. Our human side says, "forget it; I'm done." But the spiritual side says, "If Father called me to it, He would see me through it." Help us to see our pastor-husbands as You see them. Help us to know how to soothe them, encourage them, respect them, and honor them. Sometimes, Lord, the only honor they receive is from us, so help us always to be a blessing to them. Help us to recite Galatians 6:9 still to them so they can be reminded that they will reap the harvest if they faint not. In Your matchless name Jesus, I pray, Amen!

Day Eighteen

Patches to Stitch to my Life

_____

_____

_____

_____

_____

_____

_____

_____

_____

_____

_____

_____

_____

_____

_____

_____

_____

_____

_____

_____

_____

_____

_____

_____

_____

Fashion your thoughts on these:

1 Thessalonians 5:11

Ecclesiastes 4:9-12

Galatians 6:2

Heed the Warning

Put on the full armor of God so that you can take your stand against the devil's schemes.
Ephesians 6:11

When God is trying to convey a message to me, He usually will communicate it through dreams. Sometimes, these messages are warnings. In June of 2012, one month before we moved into our present location, I had an intense dream.

It occurred in our building before construction began. There was a large divider located in the middle of this large room. On the right side of the partition, there was an enormous crowd of people at a gathering of some sort. I was standing in the back of the room, watching as the people interacted with one another. It appeared that I was not visible to them. I was drawn to an image on a stage platform in a glass enclosure on the divider's left side.

The image was the most hideous yet beautiful snake that I had ever seen. It had striking bold colors of purple, gold, green, and black. Its body had a unique and ominous shape, which was large and flat. Its' head was exceedingly small, with long pointed horns that looked as if it did not belong on its body. Its body was swaying back and forth like it was following the tune of a song. As I continued to be drawn to this image, I found myself swaying along with it as if I were being hypnotized. Then out of nowhere, a faceless man suddenly appeared right by my side. He asked me if I thought the image was real. I replied, "No, of course, it's not real." He said, "look again," and when I looked back in the direction of the snake, it stopped moving and was starring directly at me. The faceless man began pushing me closer to the image to get a better look, and as I recoiled,

I said to him, "I don't do snakes!" He gave me a pensive look and said, "What are you talking about? This room is full of snakes," then he disappeared.

It was then my eyes were fully opened. I found myself in a glass enclosure that was on a swivel. As the axis turned me around, I saw the sanctuary as it is now, and snakes were everywhere. What caught my eye was this massive black snake, standing upright, hiding in a dark corner. What made me take notice was its head and its eyes. His head was large as if it didn't fit its body, and its eyes were like fire! It glared at me with such hatred that should have made me fall to my knees. I was startled but not afraid because I felt the Lord protecting me. After I woke up, I sat there praying and thinking about the meaning of this dream. I knew it was a warning.

Sister, we must be cautious as we handle the lives of people. We will encounter people who will have agendas that will appear genuine but are operating under the enemy's guise to destroy the work of the Lord and our husbands. Ensure that you are always praying for the Lord to expose the real character of those you encounter. Take heed to this, beauty can approach you in many ways, and it may be mesmerizing, but be aware it could be a snake in hiding.

Father,

Thank You for warning us of impending dangers lurking in the darkness. We are grateful that even in the dark times of ministry, You are there to protect us. In Your name, we pray, Amen!

Day Nineteen

Patches to Stitch to my Life

_____
_____
_____
_____
_____
_____
_____
_____
_____
_____
_____
_____
_____
_____
_____
_____
_____
_____
_____
_____
_____
_____
_____
_____

Fashion your thoughts on these:

Proverbs 10:9

Ephesians 5:6

1 Peter 5:8

Day Twenty

The Season of Discontent

As a prisoner for the Lord, then, I urge you to live a life worthy of the calling you have received. Be completely humble and gentle; be patient, bearing with one another in love. Make every effort to keep the unity of the Spirit through the bond of peace.
Ephesians 4:1-3

2014 was indeed a trying season for me in ministry. It seemed that I could do nothing right, especially in the eyes of people. The more I loved and gave myself, the more I was talked about, ridiculed, and lied on. I remembered the previous years of service and how I felt ministering to God's people. I gave of myself to the point of extreme exhaustion and neglect of my family. I did not allow myself to be concerned because I felt that I was doing the work of the Lord, which was to love and help His people. It became my world, my passion. I thought about ministry day and night, thinking of how I could help more, minister to the ladies in our congregation, and support my husband.

I felt like a newlywed, excited, passionate, giving, accepting, thriving, loving this new journey. However, in 2014, is when I thought that I was the only one in the relationship. It seems as if someone raised the blinds on my eyelids, and I saw that the more I gave of myself, the more it was expected. Maybe it was the exhaustion or the lack of appreciation; perhaps it was being talked about by people I gave so much to that finally opened my eyes. I am sure you can relate. You feel like you are on solid ground thriving, then suddenly you look down and see all the cracks. You thought that you were watering the ground because you were doing the work of the Lord, but the breaks kept appearing and kept getting bigger.

In September of 2014, I went to a women's retreat to be revived and prayerfully renewed. I went seeking answers as to what I am to do now. To be honest, I am not sure what I was looking for, but I found the answer in a way I did not expect. At the retreat, I felt even more unglued and detached. But in my alone time, the Lord began speaking to me. He said, "I was looking for something that man could not give me." I was empty because I took my eyes off Him and wanting my validation from others. I was so ashamed because I knew He was right.

When I got back home from the retreat, I went on a 40-day Fast to reconnect and get back in solid standing with the Lord. That experience changed my perspective on how I view ministry and God's people. The Lord strengthened me, gave me a new attitude and outlook, drew closer to my family, improved my health, and my love for ministry returned. I was able to forgive those who wronged me. When I refocused my thoughts back on Christ, He reminded me of my calling and to be patient with others. He told me that I serve Him and Him only. My job is to love His people, not to change them. I am to see others through His eyes and to help them despite themselves.

Father,

When I come to a place of discontent, help me walk in a manner you called me. You are the God who sees. It is not my job to focus on seeing; just concentrate on serving. Amen!

Day Twenty

Patches to Stitch to my Life

_____

_____

_____

_____

_____

_____

_____

_____

_____

_____

_____

_____

_____

_____

_____

_____

_____

_____

_____

_____

_____

_____

_____

_____

_____

_____

_____

Fashion your thoughts on these:

Matthew 6:33

Philippians 4:10-13

2 Corinthians 12:10

Day Twenty-One

Fashioned from the same Fabric

Then God said, "Let us make mankind in our image, in our likeness, so that they may rule over the fish in the sea and the birds in the sky, over the livestock and all the wild animals, and over all the creatures that move along the ground."
Genesis 1:26

I guess you could say that I am one who loves projects. One of my talents is creativity. If a project presents itself, whether it's a monthly theme in my classroom, a church event, or redecorating my house, I envision it and then make it a reality.

Please allow me to walk you through my vision of a project. First, I determine what the project will be, and I envision how I want the room to look. If it's decorating a place in my house, I look at my home's schematic theme. I look at the décor that already exists because the room I am decorating must coincide with the rest of the house. After I determine the colors, I take a trip to my favorite craft store, Hobby Lobby! Visiting Hobby Lobby to me is like a child seeing a toy store. I walk down each aisle, scouting out all the items that I can use in my project.

One of my favorite sections in Hobby Lobby is fabric. I carefully peruse each fabric section looking intently for the right spool to use. One of the things that I notice about each reel of material is the design patterns. Regardless of the design of the model, there is a backdrop of which the fabric is woven. For example, some models will have squares, diamonds, paisley, and animal prints, but the material's context is usually the same color or texture. And if you notice each design on the backdrop of the material, the designs can be facing outward and some inward; some are sewn on the fabric, and some are glued on. Some can be circles in one section, and some squares in another part of the material. What's significant is that the designer saw each design's uniqueness that was placed on the fabric.

God said, "He wanted to make humanity in the likeness of Him, in His image." *Barnes Commentary* says that *image* refers to outward appearance, even if the material is different. *Likeness* refers to the resemblance of any quality. Our uniqueness is that we are fashioned from Him but given unusual gifts. We are pastor's wives, but we are teachers, evangelists, worship leaders, musicians, administrators, women's ministry directors, and so much more. Our giftedness is different, but God is our backdrop.

Father,

Teach us, Lord, to walk in our true giftedness. All that matters is that Your name is glorified! In Your name, I pray, Amen!

Day Twenty-One

Patches to Stitch to my Life

_____

_____

_____

_____

_____

_____

_____

_____

_____

_____

_____

_____

_____

_____

_____

_____

_____

_____

_____

_____

_____

_____

_____

Fashion your thoughts on these:

2 Peter 4:10

Romans 12:6

1 Corinthians 12: 1-14; 40

Twenty-One, Fifty-Six

Do not let any unwholesome talk come out of your mouths, but only what is helpful for building others up according to their needs, that it may benefit those who listen.
Ephesians 4:29

I was in Walmart buying last-minute items for our 4th of July celebration. I was thinking about my daughter and how I could encourage her during this season of her life. She recently married and was now expecting their first child in January. She had been so sick and somewhat discouraged. I thought of how I could encourage her in her marriage's newness and let her know that I will always be her biggest supporter. I wanted to gently remind her that even though she was preparing to be a mother, she is a wife first. It was a conversation that I deemed delicate because of her present state, so I had to be gentle in my approach.

As I was completing my shopping, I saw two dresses valued at $9.96 each. With tax included, the total came to $21.56. I thought that she needed comfortable dresses now that the weather was warming up, and she was beginning to show in her pregnancy. So, I picked up the dresses and proceeded to check out.

When I got home, she saw me put the bag with the dresses inside on the couch. She stared at the bag and then she asked, what was in the bag? I told her to come and sit on the couch because I wanted to talk to her. She immediately became tense because she was not sure why I wanted to talk to her. I gave her the bag and told her I saw the summer dresses, and I wanted her to have something cool to wear. Her face softened, which opened the door for us to talk about married life and life in general. I began the conversation by saying that "because I am your mom, I will do anything in my power to make sure that you have everything that you need. No one will love you and be there for you like your mother." She teared up and looked at me and said, "thank you, mom."

Pastor's children must know that we are their mothers first. We pour so much into others, and we usually do it with a gentle hand. We are quick to build up others by any means necessary, and our children sometimes can get lost in the shuffle. Ministry is time-consuming and often weary at times. We are so consumed with our congregants and their needs; we sometimes forget our children need us just as much. If this is you, and you need to have a heart to heart with your precious child, do something sweet for them first. Sometimes, it only takes twenty-one dollars and fifty-six cents to break the barrier and open their hearts.

Father,

Help us always to build up our first blessings, our children. They share this walk with us. Amen!

Day Twenty-Two

Patches to Stitch to my Life

_____

_____

_____

_____

_____

_____

_____

_____

_____

_____

_____

_____

_____

_____

_____

_____

_____

_____

_____

_____

_____

_____

_____

_____

_____

Fashion your thoughts on these:

1 Thessalonians 5:11

Romans 15:2

Philippians 2:1-4

Day Twenty-Three

A Season of Pause

I consider that our present sufferings are not worth comparing with the glory that will be revealed in us.
Romans 8:18

One night as I was preparing to go to bed, I had so much on my mind. I was struggling with immediate decisions that needed to be made. As I was dosing off to sleep, I remember asking the Lord to speak to me and make it simple as to what I was supposed to do. When I finally went to sleep, I had a disturbing dream.

I dreamt that I had taken a position to teach at another school. I remember taking the children to lunch or chapel when we received a warning that a tornado was approaching. As we collaborated in the hall, I was told that this storm was one like no other, which would be disastrous. Not only was I scared, but I remembered looking at my surroundings and feeling like I had an out-of-body experience. It was chaos everywhere I looked. People were running, children were screaming, and I was standing, watching the world around me panic. As the dream progressed, the scene switched to me standing in front of a house, and I assumed it was mine. I remember my husband standing at the door and reaching out his hand to me. He said, "honey, we need to take cover now!" As I touched his hand and preparing to go inside for safety, I looked up at the storm as it was approaching, and I knew it was going to be a storm like I had never seen before. I had never seen such angry black clouds rolling in the air as I saw the ones approaching me.

I had that dream in October of 2017. I thought I had figured out what the dream meant back then. However, it was not until the middle of March of 2020, when the Lord gave me the meaning of the dream. The storm that he had forewarned me of was a virus that would affect our country and the entire world. Life as we knew it would never be the same.

I have been scared, and my anxiety has heightened. I have panicked and, at times, felt hopeless. The enemy has been using my mind as his playground to break me so that the purpose of God will not go forth. I am sure, dear sister, you may feel inadequate. You feel as if your life has stopped or, perhaps, think that it is over. I am here to tell you that your life has just begun. What is God telling you in this season? During this COVID-19 season, He has allowed everything around us to "pause." God has pushed the pause button on our life's recording systems. Now that he has paused the world for us let's push the go button and run to a higher level in him. Don't allow your mind to stall in fear and panic.

Father,

This season of waiting and uncertainty has brought our lives to a pause. We pause to say Thank You for giving us this season. It is a season where we will seek, rest, and recover. And after we have recovered, we will go forth more polished and ready to serve. In the name of Jesus, Amen!

Day Twenty-Three

Patches to Stitch to my Life

_____

_____

_____

_____

_____

_____

_____

_____

_____

_____

_____

_____

_____

_____

_____

_____

_____

_____

_____

_____

_____

_____

_____

_____

_____

_____

_____

Fashion your thoughts on these:

Daniel 2:21

Acts 1:7

1 Peter 1:6

Day Twenty-Four

Thriving While Persecuted

All this is evidence that God's judgment is right, and as a result, you will be counted worthy of the kingdom of God, for which you are suffering. God is just: He will pay back trouble to those who trouble you
2 Thessalonians 1:5-6

Kenneth and I have a running joke; "Ministry would be easier if we didn't have to deal with difficult people!" Difficult people often persecute us with their negativity, and sometimes, outright lies. We often ask ourselves, how can we thrive in a challenging environment? How can we continue to show the love of Jesus to people we know who have smiled in our faces but try to figure out how to take our places? How can we continue to serve when we have been wrongly accused of circumstances of which we were not aware? I am sure you are thinking; I can add more to this list. But truthfully, there is no thriving in ministry if we do not have a godly focus.

What things are we thinking about to thrive? Paul tells us in a letter that he wrote to the church at Philippi. Paul was thriving while persecuted because he wrote this letter in prison. In Philippians 4: 8-9, Paul says, "And now, dear brothers and sisters, one final thing. Fix your thoughts on what is true, and honorable, and right, and pure, and lovely, and admirable. Think about things that are excellent and worthy of praise. Keep putting into practice all you learned and received from me—everything you heard from me and saw me doing. Then the God of peace will be with you." We may not be physically locked in a cell as Paul was, but we may be in the prison of our minds due to the persecution we have endured. If Paul did not have a godly focus, there is no way he could, in his power and strength, encourage the church at Philippi. Because he was free in his mind, he could carry out the purpose afforded to him.

Let us thrive because this maybe for the good of someone else. Let us thrive because our focus should not be on what people think or how they respond. Let us thrive because the Kingdom is ripe for new souls that are searching for the truth. Let us thrive because even in weakness, we are made secure through the power of the Lord Jesus Christ. Let us focus on the King rather than His subjects because His reward far exceeds persecution.

Father,

Help us to keep our minds steady on You. Help us remember that even when we are being persecuted, we are thriving because our help comes from You. Amen!

Day Twenty-Four

Patches to Stitch to my Life

_____
_____
_____
_____
_____
_____
_____
_____
_____
_____
_____
_____
_____
_____
_____
_____
_____
_____
_____
_____
_____
_____

Fashion your thoughts on these:

2 Timothy 3:12

2 Corinthians 12:10

Matthew 5:10-12

It's Pruning Season

For, before the harvest, when the blossom is gone and the flower becomes a ripening grape, He will cut off the shoots with pruning knives, and cut down and take away the spreading branches.
Isaiah 18:5

Every ministry will go through a season of pruning. Our pruning season was in 2016. It seemed as if the bottom of the floor dropped from underneath us. Members of our seemly thriving congregation started leaving. Some reasons were valid, and some we did not receive. During the time of those departures, we were hurt, confused, and numb. We started questioning God of whether we should continue to endure or seek another ministry.

During one of my quiet times, the Lord reminded me of what happens when a garden is pruned. For something fresh and new to come up out of the ground, the weeds must be pulled out so the seed that has been planted can be revealed and bring forth what was intended to grow. Weeds can smother growth, which is why pruning is necessary.

Dear one, do not fret over those who leave for whatever reason. Instead, pray for them, pray for their success, pray that they find the ministry they need for them to grow. Pruning is not a bad thing; it is a necessary thing. Without pruning, flourishing is impossible. Don't let your blessings stay hidden underneath the weeds. Instead, let the Lord pull them out, so the benefits He has for you and His church will spring forth. Trust the process, believe the promises He made to you. Most of all, believe the Promise Keeper! There is no losing in God's Kingdom, so let the pruning season begin!

Father,

I realize that pruning can hurt, but spiritual growth must come forth. Help us to see the harvest instead of focusing on the weeds. Help us to remember that pruning is a process that can be painful. It is not one we would like to go through, but you must pluck the weeds so that the seeds can push through fertile soil. Amen!

Day Twenty-Five

Patches to Stitch to my Life

_____

_____

_____

_____

_____

_____

_____

_____

_____

_____

_____

_____

_____

_____

_____

_____

_____

_____

_____

_____

_____

_____

_____

_____

Fashion your thoughts on these:

John 15:2

Isaiah 43:19

Psalm 37:18-19

Time to Reflect

He says, "Be still, and know that I am God;
I will be exalted among the nations,
I will be exalted in the earth."
Psalm 46:10

I arise every morning at around 6 am. By the time my feet hit the floor, I am moving until it's time for bed. I get ready for work, I leave for work, I arrive at work, and you guessed, I go to work. While I am at work, my mind is going in so many directions. I am teaching my students, and at the same time, I am thinking about my family. I am thinking of my husband's needs, my children's needs, my mom's needs, and maybe if I have the time, I will consider my own.

Somewhere in my mind, I will think about the church and its needs. *Don't forget you have bible study on Wednesday, and yes, you must come right back for choir rehearsal on Thursday.* And as the seasons change, I am occupied with decorating the church. It is always something that distracts me from thinking of why I fell in love with ministry in the first place. I ask myself, when will you just sit, be still, and ponder the moments of what church means to you? When will you take a nice walk on a crisp, chilly day, or sit on the patio early in the morning and drink a cup of roasted coffee and just reflect?

If I truly allow my mind to be still and reflect on God's goodness, I will quickly remember why I fell in love with ministry. I would think about how many years we have been doing the church's work by ministering to God's people. Couples who were on the brink of a divorce reconciled. Those in the hospital and nursing homes encouraged me despite their infirmities. And what about when the doors of the building should have been closed? The Lord graciously commanded that they were to remain open. And let me not forget the times when we volunteered at shelters, food pantries, and talk with the recipients and witness their faith in Jesus that He would make everything alright for them in His timing. As I am writing, I reflect on a sermon my husband preached, "Pursuit Equals Value." What I pursue is what I will value the most. That sermon reminds me that my Father sought me with an intentional love even when He knew I would make a mess of my life, ignore Him at times, and just be plain ungrateful of His goodness. Yet, He valued me so much that He came down in human form and pursued me all the way to the cross! This pursuit is what I should reflect on daily to remind myself why I fell in love with ministry. I love ministry because I love my Father!

So sweet lady, when ministry seems as if it has you in constraints.; when you feel the cuffs tighten on your wrist to a point where the pain is unbearable, take a deep breath, stand still and remember how worthy He thought you were to do what He has called you to do. Reflect on His grace, his mercy, but most of all, His unexplainable love!

Father,

Thank You for the reminder that if I remain still, I can reflect on why I exalt You! In your name, I pray, Amen!

Day Twenty-Six

Patches to Stitch to my Life

_____
_____
_____
_____
_____
_____
_____
_____
_____
_____
_____
_____
_____
_____
_____
_____
_____
_____
_____
_____
_____
_____
_____
_____
_____

Fashion your thoughts on these:

Psalm 100:3

1 Chronicles 29:11

Psalm 57:5

How is your Soil

I planted the seed, Apollos watered it, but God has been making it grow.
I Corinthians 3:6

I love the color of soil, especially when it's soggy. Its rich, dark color and fresh aroma make me want to reach deep into the earth and feel its softness. For something substantial, or something of value to grow, some steps must be followed before the process of planting can begin.

When I was a young girl, I would watch my great uncle bring his tractor to my grandmother's garden in the back yard to till the soil. Using his tractor, an attachment called a box blade would break the hard ground into pieces. After the land was broken entirely, he would use the furrowing plow to create the rows. The next morning my grandmother would take a hose to the garden, use her sprinkler attachment, and set the extension in the middle of the garden. She would turn on the water and leave it on all day. I would just sit on the back porch watching the hose move all over the garden until the entire ground was wet. After the soil was soggy, she would take a hoe to each row and create holes to plant the seeds in. She explained that if the ground is dry, the seeds that are planted will not take root. They would just sit there and die. She said that when the soil is soggy enough, we can go into the garden and plant the seeds because they will sink deep into the ground and take root. Momma said after planting the seeds, they would need sunlight and water to flourish and grow. And at the right time, the seeds will begin to sprout up and produce the harvest of what was planted.

Is our soil dry and cracking because we rely on others to do what God has instructed us to do? Are our seeds sitting on top of the ground waiting for us to water it with God's love and His word? Are you putting in little work yet expecting an abundant harvest? Are we exhibiting unwavering faith as we prepare for the harvest?

The growth of the church depends on this same process. If we expect change, we must break up the hard ground so that the seeds will take root. We must take our box blade of love to break through the hard surface of hardened hearts. We must furrow through the layers of their soul by teaching them the accurate Word of God. We must water and give sunlight to encourage them, honor them, respect them, and show them their value so that the planted seeds will take root and sprout a harvest for Christ to use. When we follow the preparation steps, we are essentially telling God, I have prepared my soil, watered, and planted the seeds. I am now waiting for You to produce a harvest that will serve and grow your Kingdom.

Father,

Thank You for explicit instructions on preparing for a harvest. We may have experienced crop failures due to the lack of preparation, but You remind us that you give the increase. Our job is to prepare. Amen!

Day Twenty-Seven

Patches to Stitch to my Life

_____

_____

_____

_____

_____

_____

_____

_____

_____

_____

_____

_____

_____

_____

_____

_____

_____

_____

_____

_____

_____

_____

_____

_____

Fashion your thoughts on these:

1 Corinthians 3:7

Matthew 13:30

Proverbs 24:27

Reset Awakening

Therefore, if anyone is in Christ, the new creation has come:[a] The old has gone,
the new is here!
2 Corinthians 5:17

I love playing games on my IPAD. It is my time to unwind from the stress that I endure each day. One day my daughter used my IPAD and forgot to log out of it. After logging her out and preparing to log in under my name, I suddenly forgot my password. I attempted three times to remember the password but could not, and as a result, I was locked out of my IPAD. The only solution was to wipe it clean, reset it, and start over.

I stewed over this for months because I did not want to wipe my IPAD clean. I could not remember everything that I had on it, and I was afraid to clean it because I did not want to lose any of my data, whether it was valuable or not. Finally, I resolved that If I ever wanted to use my IPAD again, I had to reset it and begin again. So, I started the painstaking process of wiping it clean. The exciting thing was that during this process, I did not lose as much as I thought that I would. What I thought I had lost and valued was still there, and what I did not need was wiped clean. I found it easy to replace what I lost, clean out what I did not need, and begin again. I stopped focusing on what I could not hold onto and allowed myself to open up to what I could gain.

Ministry is pretty much the same way my sweet PW sister. Sometimes God must lock the program that we were so comfortable in and wipe our system of comfort clean so that we can begin again. We may never know what new creations are available to us because we are afraid that God will scrub over programs we want to keep and wiped them clean. We need to trust Him to show us our mistakes with the old ministry systems and allow Him to develop new methods in our ministry. He wants to wipe us clean so that we can start again in a new and improved setting. Awaken my sister and RESET!

Father,

I must admit that I sometimes get too comfortable in my current setting. I have to admit that sometimes You have to lock the door so that I can seek You to open another. Help me not to become complacent in my thinking, but instead look to You to develop new creations through me. In Your name, I pray, Amen!

Day Twenty-Eight

Patches to Stitch to my Life

_____

_____

_____

_____

_____

_____

_____

_____

_____

_____

_____

_____

_____

_____

_____

_____

_____

_____

_____

_____

_____

_____

_____

_____

_____

_____

_____

Fashion your thoughts on these:

Isaiah 43:18-19

Isaiah 42:9

Ezekiel 36:26

Day Twenty-Nine

There is Ministry in Your Presence

Carry each other's burdens, and in this way, you will fulfill the law of Christ.
Galatians 6:2

January 22, 2018, will be a day that is etched in my brain for the rest of my life. At 5:40 a.m., my husband and I received a phone call from dear friends we have known for over 30 years. Their first-born 26-year-old son was unresponsive, and they needed us to pray. We immediately got out of bed and fell to our knees with an urgent plea to God to spare his life. After we prayed, I waited 45 minutes before I texted my friend to get an update and to let her know that prayers would continue for their son. She immediately texted me back and said, "He is with Jesus now." It felt as if someone reached down into my lungs and sucked all the air from them. How would I tell my children who grew up with him that he had passed away suddenly? This was unbearable pain.

Our friends were in Houston when they received the news about their son, who lived in Oklahoma with his wife. They had to drive back to Jackson, Mississippi to pick up their remaining two children, then travel to Oklahoma to be with their daughter in law. My husband and I decided to drive to Oklahoma and be with them.

So many thoughts were swimming around in my head as we were traveling. My friend and I had been texting back and forth; she questioned why this had happened to her son. I simply could not answer. What do you say to a mother who just lost her first-born child? How can I tell her God's Word of which she knows? How could I tell her I know how she feels when I did not? I could not understand her pain, her sorrow, her grief. I remembered something

89

my husband said a long time ago, "Sometimes all people need from you is to be there and help them cry." After we connected with them, that is precisely what we did, we helped our friends cry, and we listened to them. Another pastor's wife, who was there, made a profound statement to me. She said, "There is ministry in your presence." That resonated deeply in my soul because it confirmed that I was right where God needed me to be. I did not have the words or answers, but my presence spoke more volumes than my lips. She needed me to hold her hand, to hug her, to listen, and just be there.

Dear one, you will not be able to answer some questions or offer explanations during a tragedy. But your presence will prove to be robust and trust me, it will be enough.

Father,

Thank You for reminding me that my silence is a form of ministry. I may not have the words to comfort loved ones or friends, but I am thankful my presence speaks volumes. In Your name, I pray, Amen!

Day Twenty-Nine

Patches to Stitch to my Life

_____

_____

_____

_____

_____

_____

_____

_____

_____

_____

_____

_____

_____

_____

_____

_____

_____

_____

_____

_____

_____

_____

_____

_____

Fashion your thoughts on these:

Hebrew 10:24-25

Galatians 6:1

John 13:34

Day Thirty

Your First Ministry

If anyone does not know how to manage his own family, how can he take care of God's church?
1 Timothy 3:5

It's time. Those are the words my husband heard when he was called to pastor a church. He had heard those same two words when he was called to preach, and now, the Lord confirmed those words again that He was called to do more excellent work.

Ministry is a consumer. It consumes your mind, your heart, your spirit, your body, and your soul. Only God can equip a body and a heart to handle the pressures of church ministry. And honestly, only God can prepare a body and mind to juggle both a family and a church. However, while we are juggling, remember the first toss goes to the ministry of family.

When I think back to my husband being called to pastor, I remind myself that our entire family unit was called as well. While we do not hold the office of a pastor, our whole family has been gifted to serve in the capacity that God has selected. The family of the pastor must be a pleasant and productive unit first. If they are not, they can very well become unhealthy last family. The first family is the last family to fellowship together. The last to be comforted. The last to be noticed. The last to take care of themselves. The last to have their concerns addressed. The last to be recognized for their faithful service and the last for others to see the pain and sorrow in their eyes. The first family is not just a church recognizable family, but a family who leads by example of honoring God first.

Dear one, there is an adage that I am convinced Satan himself strategically spoke into existence that some of the worst kids are pastors and teachers' kids. I would like to boldly speak against this lie because my husband and I have worked hard to show our children and others that our family is our priority no matter what is going on in the church. Never let the church take you away from the first ministry God has trusted you with, your family. They are not just the first family of your church; they are your first family.

Father,

Thank You for the reminder that my most precious first ministry is to my family. Let me not forget how valuable they are to me because they are relevant to You. In Your name, I pray, Amen!

Day Thirty

Patches to Stitch to my Life

_____
_____
_____
_____
_____
_____
_____
_____
_____
_____
_____
_____
_____
_____
_____
_____
_____
_____
_____
_____
_____
_____
_____
_____

Fashion your thoughts on these:

1 Peter 3:7

1 Timothy 3:5

Titus 2:1-15

The Galatians 6:10 Project

Therefore, as we have opportunity, let us do good to all people, especially to those who belong to the family of believers.
Galatians 6:10

As a child growing up in Jackson, Mississippi, I, along with my childhood friend, would ride along with my grandmother and her mother to visit the church's sick and shut-in. I cannot begin to tell you the impact these visitations had on my life. We would watch our mothers buy and cook food and freeze meals so that these precious members would have enough food to eat. My friend and I could not cook because we were too young, but we would clean their houses until they smelled like Pine-Sol throughout. Afterward, we would sit at the feet of these precious souls and listen to their hearts. They would tell us how their children and grandchildren had forsaken them by not coming to visit them. It brought all of us to tears. They would have tears in their eyes when they expressed their gratitude to us for thinking enough about them to come and serve. Our church in Mississippi was and is still significant in helping those who are in need.

After leaving Mississippi, the spirit of servanthood remained with me because this was the true meaning of showing love one to another. Not only did we minister to the sick, but if a neighbor was visiting during the time of our arrival, we had the opportunity to minister to them as well. Serving others shows us how deeply blessed we are.

In November of 2015, after seven years of our church being in existence, it resonated in my heart again to start a service evangelism ministry to those who were sick, caregivers, depressed, grieving, and those who had just given birth. For those who could not make it to church, we would take the church to them. We had the opportunity to read scripture, sing songs of praise, pray, and just visit with them. If they had other needs, we would offer to take care of whatever was needed so that they could heal, be encouraged, and, most of all, know that they had not been forgotten. I cannot begin to tell you how it blessed the recipients, and it blessed those of us who were able to visit. The church isn't just about what we receive on Sunday mornings; it is what we can take away from it and give to others.

Father,

I am honored to serve You. It is my service to others that shows I am doing the work of the church. In Your name, I pray, Amen!

Day Thirty-One

Patches to Stitch to my Life

_____
_____
_____
_____
_____
_____
_____
_____
_____
_____
_____
_____
_____
_____
_____
_____
_____
_____
_____
_____
_____
_____
_____

Fashion your thoughts on these:

Hebrews 13:16

Philippians 2:4

Proverbs 19:17

Purpose or Programs

Many are the plans in a person's heart, but it is the LORD's purpose that prevails.
Proverbs 19:21

I can remember the annual programs that took place back at my home church. Women's Day, Men's Day, Youth's Day (my favorite), Usher's Day, and Family's Day, to name a few. These programs would showcase the many talents that were displayed throughout our church. Family Day stands out the most because it was designed to see how much money each family could raise and who would have the most family members present. I am not saying that there is something wrong with having programs if the program's real intent is to minister instead of showcasing. If the event is only to stay in the traditional mode instead of reaching the lost, it is merely a program. You know what I mean; we will continue with these programs because this is what has been done for centuries. A traditional mindset is hard to reprogram. However, if the event is geared towards drawing the lost to Christ and serving humanity, it has transitioned from program to purpose.

We are living in times that people are desperate to be attached to something. Suicide is on the rise; mass shootings are on the rise; same-sex marriages have migrated and have become the norm in our society. Some people are so confused about their sexuality that they are searching through the alphabet to find a letter that suits their gender preference. The world has become more depraved, self-absorbed, and headed on a downward spiral to hell.

We can no longer be locked into the twilight zone of tradition! We must reach this delusional world through ministry events that have a purpose. A purposed event is not self-seeking, and a purposed event is not a showcase but a soul seeking case. A purposed event is not traditionally required, but Holy-Spirit inspired. A purposed event is not a display of talent only, but to transform that talent to minister to others. The next time we plan an event, let us ask ourselves, is it traditionally based or purposed based.

Father,

It is for Your purpose that I live. Please keep my mind on when I am operating in purposeful living, and souls are being saved for kingdom living. In Your name, I pray, Amen!

Day Thirty-Two

Patches to Stitch to my Life

_____

_____

_____

_____

_____

_____

_____

_____

_____

_____

_____

_____

_____

_____

_____

_____

_____

_____

_____

_____

_____

_____

Fashion your thoughts on these:

Proverbs 16:9

Ephesians 2:10

Proverbs 19:21

I am the Child; You are the Parent

> Because the Lord disciplines the one he loves,
> and he chastens everyone he accepts as his son."
> *Hebrews 12:6*

One of our favorite things to do as a family is to visit relatives in Mississippi. One afternoon at my grandmothers' house, we were all in the kitchen fixing lunch, and my son, who was a little boy at the time, wanted something that I told him he could not have. After telling him several times that he could not have what he wanted, he proceeded to throw a tantrum. During his outburst, he temporarily lost his senses! He proceeded to raise his voice, telling me he was the parent, and I was the child.

At that moment, I took on the character of Claire Huxtable from the Cosby show. I turned slowly, looked in his 4-year old little face, and asked, "WHAT did you say?" His response was priceless, and we laugh about it to this day. As he looked up at me and realized that his impromptu remark had sparked a look in my face that no child wants to see, he quickly and intelligently responded with a calmer voice, "I said, you the parent, I the child."

As parents, we are given the rights and privileges to raise our children as God intends. When a mother goes through pregnancy and giving birth to a child, her tolerance for rebellion becomes intolerable. When we think of the many things that we do and have done for our children, it is hard to hear and see tantrums and defiance. Yet, this is how we act towards God. We become temperamental when we cannot have our way, even when our way often will get us into situations we cannot escape on our own.

I imagine God giving a stern look of disapproval when he tells us, no, you cannot have what you are asking for at this time. We temporarily forget who he is. We throw tantrums, we rebel, and we talk back to him, the Creator of our souls. Can you imagine Jesus saying, "after ALL that I have done for them, they disrespect me?" Where were they when I was beaten beyond recognition? Where were they when people spit on me? Where were they when I was mocked? Where were they when I was betrayed? Where were they when those long spikes were hammered deep into my hands and feet? Where were they when I hung on that cross of shame? Where were they when I finally gave up my spirit and died, just for them?

After looking at his account, his track record of consistent love, we finally can look up again after coming to our senses, and respond intelligently and calmly, "Jesus, You are the parent, and I am the child, I repent."

Father,

Forgive us when we forget our place. Forgive us when our minds take a temporary leave of absence, and we forget all that You have done and continue to do for us. We thank You for the firm reminder that You are the parent; we are the children because You always know what is best for us. In Your name, Amen!

Day Thirty-Three

Patches to Stitch to my Life

_____

_____

_____

_____

_____

_____

_____

_____

_____

_____

_____

_____

_____

_____

_____

_____

_____

_____

_____

_____

_____

_____

Fashion your thoughts on these:

Revelation 3:19

Proverbs 3:11-12

Hebrews 12:8

You're Worth more than Your Shoes

She is clothed with strength and dignity; she can laugh at the days to come.
Proverbs 31:25

Oooh, girlfriend, I have met some sharply dressed Pastors' wives. I am talking about knowing how to put an outfit together. As a young girl, I saw the pastors' wives dressed in elegant two pieced suits and dresses, matching big hats leaning to one side covering one eye, silk scarves, handbags, and shoes setting off the entire outfit. Oh, those shoes would often catch my eye. Shoes that were uniquely crafted by a well-known designer that made the whole ensemble stand out.

During my childhood, a pastor's wife dressed impeccably because it was expected. The shoes were the selling point to set off the outfit, or whispers and gossip would move through the congregation. The church cared more about how she looked rather than the value of her heart and service.

One Sunday after service, as I was exiting the stage where I had sung with the praise team, I was approached by a parishioner regarding my shoes. I make it a point that when I am serving, I need to keep both my feet flat to the ground so that I can give my all to serving the Lord. My focus is not to be cute but to exhibit purpose in what I am called to do. After completing the singing mission that Sunday, I changed into another pair of shoes to go and fellowship alongside my husband to greet the members and visitors. This parishioner walked up to me as I was prepared to go into the fellowship hall and said, "I am so glad that you changed out of those ugly shoes you were wearing on stage." And if that was not enough, she continued by saying. "I was looking at your shoes, and I said to myself, I sure hope she has better shoes than that." I responded by saying, "I could not have given my all if my shoes were cute, so I needed to have ugly shoes on to praise the Lord freely."

I wondered why a congregation couldn't look beyond the pastor's wife's feet to see her true worth. Does this amazing woman of God know that her value is in her heart and not on her feet? Girlfriend, no one likes to strut her style more than me. However, my style is not the forerunner of my character. In times past, pastors' wives were seen and not heard. Her only role was to sit on a shelf like a porcelain doll and be admired. Today, a pastor's wife can wear the blinging shoes and use those same shoes to walk in her calling value. Take your eyes off the shoes and look where the feet in them are going.

Father,

Let my blinging shoes lead me to witness to others who desperately need You. Help me to see that this is what You value. In Your name, I pray, Amen!

Day Thirty-Four

Patches to Stitch to my Life

_____

_____

_____

_____

_____

_____

_____

_____

_____

_____

_____

_____

_____

_____

_____

_____

_____

_____

_____

_____

_____

_____

_____

_____

_____

_____

Fashion your thoughts on these:

1 Timothy 2:9

Proverbs 31:30

1 Peter 3:3-8

An Abundance Coming from Blood

For I know the plans I have for you," declares the LORD, "plans to prosper you and not to harm you, plans to give you hope and a future.
Jeremiah 29:11

Seven months after giving birth to my first child while living in Fairfax, Virginia, we decided that we needed a vacation, so we traveled to Mississippi to visit our families. I was experiencing a mild case of post-partum depression and was feeling overwhelmed as a new mother. I was so afraid of failing that it caused me to become detached from the world around me.

While we stayed at my grandmother's house, my husband, me, and the baby decided to nap. As I fell asleep, I started crying and praying to the Lord about His purpose for my life. I felt empty inside, and I wondered if He had a plan for us as a family and for me. I went to sleep, praying, and the Lord answered me immediately in a dream.

My husband, the baby, and I were standing in front of a trench in my dream. I was pregnant again, and my husband was holding our son. What caught my attention was people standing in front of an ocean with fishing rods to my far left. I remember the water being so blue that it was transparent. But the people holding the fishing rods stood there like robots or zombies. People standing in front of crystal blue water with the fishing rods stood like dead men.

Meanwhile, my husband and I were holding fishing rods standing in front of this trench. I looked down into the channel and exclaimed to my husband, "Look at how dirty and bloody this water is. How can anything be alive in this?" Then suddenly, I threw my rod into the water and caught two fish. My husband did the same, and he caught four fish. We both kept throwing our rods into this bloody, dirty water, and each time, we caught multiple fish on our lines, then I woke up.

When we return to Virginia, I met with our pastor to tell him about my dream. He smiled at me and said, "First, you are going to have another baby. And what God was showing you was that you both would catch harvest of souls." The dirt represents the sin, and the blood represents Christ's sacrifice on the cross." He then looked at my husband and said, "Son, don't go until He calls you."

Years later, 28, to be exact, we could not see down the road the plan the Lord had for us. All we know and believe is we are right where the Lord wants us, and we are walking in our destiny. He has shown us too much for us to doubt Him now.

I do not know what God has shown you. But I want to encourage you to continue to press forward and work faithfully for His Kingdom. In due time, His plan will manifest itself, and the promises of what He has shown you will surely come to pass.

Father,

It is in Your time that You will manifest the blessing. Help me to be ready when You do. In Your name, I pray, Amen!

Day Thirty-Five

Patches to Stitch to my Life

_____
_____
_____
_____
_____
_____
_____
_____
_____
_____
_____
_____
_____
_____
_____
_____
_____
_____
_____
_____
_____
_____
_____
_____

Fashion your thoughts on these:

Jeremiah 1:5

Romans 8:28

Proverbs 3:5-6

Day Thirty-Six

Life on Hold

Yes, my soul, find rest in God; my hope comes from him.
Psalm 62:5

No one could have convinced me that on March 10, 2020, I would enter Life's holding cell. This day was during my spring break, a time of rest from my precious preschool children. I was supposed to return recharged and preparing for the end of the school year. Instead, I found myself on lockdown in my house due to a global pandemic that had invaded our country.

Like you, I was filled with various kinds of emotions and fears. The more I read about this virus and its potentially deadly effects, the more unglued I became. I was not only quarantined in my house, but my mind was in solitary. The more I gave into fear, the more it beckoned for me.

One morning as I was preparing to surf the internet, I heard the voice of God say to me, "You complained to Me about being too busy to write. You said that you had so much on your plate that you did not have the energy to do anything when you got home. Now that I have put life as you knew it on hold, what is your excuse now?" I sat there for a moment and thought to myself, God is right. I have no more excuses because He has freed my schedule and my mind. That moment brought a stillness to my soul. He wanted me to be still. My purpose was not put on hold because I was sheltered in place; instead, the lockdown created an opportunity for me to busy myself even more for His kingdom.

Waiting during turbulent times can be trying and downright frightening. I would envision in my mind how the children of Israel felt when they were quarantined inside, waiting for death to pass over. I know they trusted God, and they believed Moses, but being human can overtake logic if we allow it. I could feel their fear, see them trembling in my mind wondering if death would pass over them. But the one thing that emerged in my mind was the blood over the doorpost. I thought about Jesus and the blood that He shed for me. His blood covers not only me but my entire household. The children of Israel may have been reluctant, but they obeyed and went inside and closed the door. So, while I am waiting for God to bring this virus to its knees, I am waiting quietly in Him. But quietly waiting does not mean to refrain; it means to continue working while waiting.

Father,

Waiting for storms to pass can make us uneasy, but when our hope is in You, our focus changes because we know that You have secured us in You. Thank You, Lord, for not only keeping my body but preserving my mind. In Your name, I pray, Amen!

Day Thirty-Six

Patches to Stitch to my Life

_____

_____

_____

_____

_____

_____

_____

_____

_____

_____

_____

_____

_____

_____

_____

_____

_____

_____

_____

_____

_____

_____

_____

_____

_____

Fashion your thoughts on these:

Romans 12:12

Isaiah 40:31

Psalm 39:7

Day Thirty-Seven

Constricted Silence

Do not be anxious about anything, but in every situation, by prayer and petition, with thanksgiving, present your requests to God. And the peace of God, which transcends all understanding, will guard your hearts and your minds in Christ Jesus.
Philippians 4:6-7

From the time I was a child, I have experienced anxiety and fear. I am sure growing up in a loving yet, pessimistic home is attributed to much of this. I remember overhearing a conversation from members of my family that we were perhaps cursed. They agreed that a curse was on our family because each of their siblings, including them, had lost a child or a grandchild tragically. I was around seven or eight years old, and this had a devastatingly profound effect on me. I remembered walking up to my grandmother sobbing, and I asked her if I would die. She pulled me close to her and said, "No, baby, you are not going to die."

Years had passed since I had that conversation with my grandmother, but those cunning spirits of anxiety and fear took residence inside my soul that day. Every life event after that conversation made me an inmate in the prison of my mind. I questioned everything, and no answer could satisfy me. Growing up, I saw tragedy after tragedy in my family and often wondered, would I be next. There were times I could not empathically express my feelings because my vocal cords would constrict to keep me in a place of silence. I did not understand until I was older and had spiritually grown that it was the enemy who sent an agent in my younger years to arrest my mind and put it in fear's prison. I was held there for years until I *believed* that Jesus paid the price for my release.

As a pastor's wife, we are usually on the front lines telling others how to be released from anxiety and fear. Yet, we are battling fears we are ashamed to admit. We are not exempt from life, dear lady; we have been called to a higher work despite life. So how can we move forward when we experience ongoing battles in our minds? Confess it openly. The enemy wants to silence you. He has a moment by moment conversation with your mind daily. You listen to this exchange until it has manifested itself in your heart, then it becomes a matter of the heart. When you speak out against it, the magnitude of fear starts dissipating, and you began to walk in freedom. After confession, listen, read, and walk in the Word of God. Let it be the salve to your soul. Be consumed with Jesus and submit to His authority. He will release you from the spirit of fear.

Father,

We are living in uncertain times that change second by second. You are the only consistency in our lives. Help us remember that if we remain close to you, our minds will always be on you. And if our minds have waited on you, the spirit of fear will die because we have stopped giving it the power to operate. In Your name Jesus, I pray, Amen!

Day Thirty-Seven

Patches to Stitch to my Life

_____
_____
_____
_____
_____
_____
_____
_____
_____
_____
_____
_____
_____
_____
_____
_____
_____
_____
_____
_____
_____
_____
_____
_____

Fashion your thoughts on these:

Isaiah 41:10

2 Timothy 1:7

Joshua 1:9

The Leaning Oak

Rooted and built up in him, strengthened in the faith as you were taught, and
overflowing with thankfulness.
Colossians 2:7

On my way to and from my job, I usually take the same route, Custer, to Renner Road. As I was traveling home from my job this day, I arrived at the intersection of Custer and Spring Creek and stopped at the traffic light. Like many of you, I usually look around to pass the time and wait for the light to change. As I was looking around, I noticed an oak tree. I had seen this tree many times, but what caught my attention was the tall oak was leaning down towards the ground. Its roots were firmly embedded in the environment stabilizing the tree. I thought to myself, how in the world did I not see this before. As I sat starring at the tree, even though its branches were facing down, it was not touching the ground. Its strong roots secured the tree deep into the earth so that its branches remained steady.

As I drove off, I thought about how our faith should be. We, as pastors' wives, are often faced with difficult challenges in our ministry. We often spread ourselves thin doing one task after another one. And it does not help when we feel that what we do is not being appreciated but instead criticized. But like this oak, our roots are embedded deep in the faith of our Savior, Jesus Christ. When He called us, He started securing our hearts to withstand the many challenges we would face in ministry. And just like that oak, we may lean at times, but we will never touch the ground because our Father has rooted us deep in Him so that we can continue to carry out the purpose and plans He has for us.

My dear sister, don't allow the enemy to whisper in your ear that you are not doing what you have been called to do. Don't let him put a shadow over your mind so that you feel that you will fall to the ground. When the enemy charges at you, remind him that on Christ the Solid Rock you stand. All other ground is sinking sand! You will lean, but He will keep you from hitting the ground. He has anchored you. Pace yourself and keep going!

Father,

Thank You for anchoring our roots deeply in You. We know that life can hit us so hard that we find ourselves leaning to the ground. We are grateful to know that Your anchor holds, and it will keep us from falling. In Your name, I pray, Amen!

Day Thirty-Eight

Patches to Stitch to my Life

_____
_____
_____
_____
_____
_____
_____
_____
_____
_____
_____
_____
_____
_____
_____
_____
_____
_____
_____
_____
_____
_____
_____
_____
_____
_____

Fashion your thoughts on these:

Ephesians 6:10

1 Corinthians 16:13

1 Chronicles 16:11

I Get It

Likewise, teach the older women to be reverent in the way they live, not to be slanderers or addicted to much wine, but to teach what is good.
Titus 2: 3

Not too long ago, my husband and I were invited to a birthday celebration for a pastor friend of ours. My first inclination was not to attend because I was simply not in a celebrating mood due to the recent passing of my Mentor. I just wanted to remain in my solitude and reflect on old times. My husband asked if I wanted to go; I hesitated at first, but we both felt I needed a change of scenery, so we went. Immediately after arriving and walking in, I felt the presence of welcoming hearts. Everyone was laughing, talking, and just loving on one another. The spirit of sadness began to dissipate as I envelop the ambiance of the environment. The music was inviting, the food was delicious, and the fellowship was pleasant.

After dinner, there was a series of tributes given to the guest of honor. Some were from other pastors, but mostly from his staff. But the one that intrigued me the most was the tribute from his wife. She stated how much he meant to her and how much their children loved and adored him. Then she looked into his eyes and said, "I get it." That statement struck a chord in my soul because, at that moment, I understood the meaning of her sentiment.

My mentor became an intricate part of my life in a short time. When I was blessed to sit at her feet, I felt the Lord's wisdom and guidance through her. She never looked at herself as I looked at her. She was a woman full of grace and humility. Here, this powerful woman of God, known all over the nation, taking time to pour into me, encourage me, and speak into my life things that I did not even see in myself. Yet, she kept pushing me, praying for me, and drawing me to herself.

After her death, I began to go back and read previous messages, comments, and videos she made. I viewed a video that I was privileged to be a part of with her, searching for an answer to what I should do now in her absence. After reading the comments and listening to the videos, I got it. I finally understood all those years of what she was saying to me and why she pushed me.

Sister, perhaps you have a mentor that is pouring into your life. She sees in you by the grace of God and his revelation of what you should be doing in ministry. Pay attention to those words, listen carefully, and look into her eyes. When you listen intently and watch through spiritual eyes, you will get it.

Father,

When we doubt why we were chosen to be a pastor's wife, allow us to remember a mentor's words that You have given to remind us. In Your name, I pray, Amen!

Day Thirty-Nine

Patches to Stitch to my Life

_____

_____

_____

_____

_____

_____

_____

_____

_____

_____

_____

_____

_____

_____

_____

_____

_____

_____

_____

_____

_____

_____

_____

Fashion your thoughts on these:

1 Peter 5:5

Hebrews 13:17

Ephesians 5:21

Day Forty

Push Until You Deliver

For we are God's handiwork, created in Christ Jesus to do good works, which God prepared in advance for us to do.
Ephesians 2:10

One of the precious times in my life is when I had the opportunity to witness the birth of my first grandchild. After my daughter was prepped for the baby's arrival, I was advised that I could stand at the end of the birthing table to watch the process of the baby being born.

My daughter was given instructions from the nurse on how she was to "push" during a contraction. As many of you know, giving birth to a child is exhausting, and a small part of you wants to give up because you feel as if the process will never come to an end. When it was time to push, my daughter wasn't bearing down in the way she had been instructed. She had not given birth before, so this process would take some time to acquire. The nurse gently explained how she was to push so that her baby would move closer and closer to the birth canal. She said, "Sweetie, this is how you must push. Bear down with all your might and release when I tell you to." After a few times, my daughter finally understood, and she started doing as she was told. When she followed the instructions, we started seeing progress.

As the baby got closer and closer to the birth canal, the nurse explained that every time my daughter stopped pushing, the baby would get suctioned back in a little. She said that it was a normal part of the process and the progression as the baby draws closer to the birth canal.

As God is birthing His purpose out of us, we sometimes resist and get sucked back into the peculiarities of life. He pushes, we move, then a distraction pops up, and we are pulled back from the very thing from which He is trying to deliver us.

What is God trying to push out of you? Are you moving towards the birth canal or still resisting? Beautiful one, do not fight. Keep moving towards the channel of your purpose so that you can enter the destiny the Father has planned for you.

Father,

Help us to remember that labor pains bring forth a glorious purpose. We may get sucked in from the vacuum of life, but we will spring forth into our destinies if we continue to push. In Your name, we pray, Amen!

Day Forty

Patches to Stitch to my Life

_____

_____

_____

_____

_____

_____

_____

_____

_____

_____

_____

_____

_____

_____

_____

_____

_____

_____

_____

_____

_____

_____

_____

_____

_____

_____

_____

Fashion your thoughts on these:

Jeremiah 1:5

Ephesians 2:10

Philippians 1:6

About the Author

Melissa West was born and raised in Jackson, Mississippi, to Jessie and Violet Shelby. She was lovingly raised and trained by her grandmother, Sarah Griffin. Melissa attended Jackson State University, where she met and married her college sweetheart, Pastor Kenneth T. West Sr., on May 14, 1988. She completed her bachelor's degree in Child Care and Family Education with a minor in Music Education. She has been an Educator and an Entrepreneur for over 20 years.

Melissa has been a Pastor's wife since 2009. She leads the Women's ministry and serves on the Praise Team at Berean Bible Fellowship Church in Plano, TX. Melissa is instrumental in helping her husband in whatever capacity is needed. In addition to serving in her church, she is a bible teacher, speaker and serves as the DFW Pastor's Wives' leader formerly under the direction and leadership of Dr. Lois Irene Evans since 2015.

Melissa is passionate about doing the work of the Lord and her family. In her spare time, she loves to read, spend time at the beach, and go to the Spa.

Melissa and her husband, Kenneth, are the proud parents of Kenneth Jr. and Muriel, their son in love Devon, and proud grandparents of Violet Grace Bonnick.

www.ingramcontent.com/pod-product-compliance
Lightning Source LLC
Chambersburg PA
CBHW070751180626
46818CB00007B/3077